"Kids always do better with a father,"

his assistant, Jeanne, insisted. "Any interest in taking on the role?"

"Hannah and I are still at the friendship stage," Eric said.

"Really? You can't tell me there isn't even a spark."

There was an entire forest fire, but he wasn't about to discuss that.

"We're friends," he said firmly. "I plan to keep things that way. Speaking of which, if you get a chance would you please put together a list of books on pregnancy?"

Jeanne raised her eyebrows. "I see."

"Don't get too excited. I want to learn what I can, so I can help out. Be there for her. As friends."

"Uh-huh. Sure. I'm convinced. None of this is because you think Hannah is hot."

He headed for his office. "I'm ignoring you."

"That doesn't make me any less right."

Dear Reader,

Well, the new year is upon us—and if you've resolved to read some wonderful books in 2004, you've come to the right place. We'll begin with *Expecting!* by Susan Mallery, the first in our five-book MERLYN COUNTY MIDWIVES miniseries, in which residents of a small Kentucky town find love—and scandal—amidst the backdrop of a midwifery clinic. In the opening book, a woman returning to her hometown, pregnant and alone, finds herself falling for her high school crush—now all grown up and married to his career! Or so he thinks....

Annette Broadrick concludes her SECRET SISTERS trilogy with *MacGowan Meets His Match.* When a woman comes to Scotland looking for a job *and* the key to unlock the mystery surrounding her family, she finds both—with the love of a lifetime thrown in!—in the Scottish lord who hires her. In *The Black Sheep Heir,* Crystal Green wraps up her KANE'S CROSSING miniseries with the story of the town outcast who finds in the big, brooding stranger hiding out in her cabin the soul mate she'd been searching for.

Karen Rose Smith offers the story of an about-to-be single mom and the handsome hometown hero who makes her wonder if she doesn't have room for just one more male in her life, in *Their Baby Bond.* THE RICHEST GALS IN TEXAS, a new miniseries by Arlene James, in which three blue-collar friends inherit a million dollars—each!—opens with *Beautician Gets Million-Dollar Tip!* A hairstylist inherits that wad just in time to bring her salon up to code, at the insistence of the infuriatingly handsome, if annoying, local fire marshal. And in Jen Safrey's *A Perfect Pair,* a woman who enlists her best (male) friend to help her find her Mr. Right suddenly realizes he's right there in front of her face—i.e., said friend! Now all she has to do is convince *him* of this....

So bundle up, and happy reading. And come back next month for six new wonderful stories, all from Silhouette Special Edition.

Sincerely,

Gail Chasan
Senior Editor

Susan Mallery

EXPECTING!

Silhouette®

SPECIAL EDITION®

Published by Silhouette Books

America's Publisher of Contemporary Romance

Special thanks and acknowledgment are given to Susan Mallery for her contribution to the MERLYN COUNTY MIDWIVES series.

To Jean—
a terrific mother, grandmother and mother-in-law

SILHOUETTE BOOKS

ISBN 0-373-24585-8

EXPECTING!

This edition published by arrangement with Harlequin Books S.A.

Visit Silhouette at www.eHarlequin.com

Printed in U.S.A.

Books by Susan Mallery

Silhouette Special Edition

Tender Loving Care #717
More Than Friends #802
A Dad for Billie #834
Cowboy Daddy #898
**The Best Bride* #933
**Marriage on Demand* #939
**Father in Training* #969
The Bodyguard & Ms. Jones #1008
**Part-Time Wife* #1027
Full-Time Father #1042
**Holly and Mistletoe* #1071
**Husband by the Hour* #1099
†*The Girl of His Dreams* #1118
†*The Secret Wife* #1123
†*The Mysterious Stranger* #1130
The Wedding Ring Promise #1190
Prince Charming, M.D. #1209
The Millionaire Bachelor #1220
‡*Dream Bride* #1231
‡*Dream Groom* #1244
Beth and the Bachelor #1263
Surprise Delivery #1273
A Royal Baby on the Way #1281
A Montana Mavericks Christmas:
"Married in Whitehorn" #1286
Their Little Princess #1298
***The Sheik's Kidnapped Bride* #1316
***The Sheik's Arranged Marriage* #1324
***The Sheik's Secret Bride* #1331
‡‡*The Rancher Next Door* #1358
‡‡*Unexpectedly Expecting!* #1370
‡‡*Wife in Disguise* #1383
Shelter in a Soldier's Arms #1400
***The Sheik and the Runaway Princess* #1430
Christmas in Whitehorn #1435
***The Sheik & the Virgin Princess* #1453
***The Prince & the Pregnant Princess* #1473
**Good Husband Material* #1501
The Summer House
"Marrying Mandy" #1510
**Completely Smitten* #1520
**One in a Million* #1543
**Quinn's Woman* #1557
A Little Bit Pregnant #1573
Expecting! #1585

Silhouette Intimate Moments

Tempting Faith #554
The Only Way Out #646
Surrender in Silk #770
Cinderella for a Night #1029

Silhouette Books

36 Hours
The Rancher and the Runaway Bride

Montana Mavericks Weddings
"Cowgirl Bride"

World's Most Eligible Bachelors
Lone Star Millionaire

Sheiks of Summer
"The Sheikh's Virgin"

Harlequin Books

Montana Mavericks: Big Sky Grooms
"Spirit of the Wolf"

Harlequin Historicals

Justin's Bride #270
Wild West Wife #419
Shotgun Grooms #575
"Lucas's Convenient Bride"

*Hometown Heartbreakers
†Triple Trouble
‡Brides of Bradley House
**Desert Rogues
‡‡Lone Star Canyon

SUSAN MALLERY

is the bestselling and award-winning author of over fifty books for Harlequin and Silhouette Books. She makes her home once again in California with her handsome prince of a husband and her two adorable-but-not-bright cats.

Merlyn County Regional

Hospital Happenings

Congratulations to Geoff Bingham for securing the first round of funding for the hospital's latest endeavor—a state-of-the-art biomedical research facility. And thanks to the South Junction Beautification Committee for beginning the clean-up of the location for the new center. We appreciate the planting of those rosebushes, ladies!

Dr. Mari Bingham is still accepting volunteers for work in the Foster Midwifery Clinic. From cuddling babies to mailing fund-raising letters for the new research facility, Mari would love your help! Contact the Foster Clinic reception area for more information.

Finally, on a more personal note, everyone's favorite hospital director, that flirtatious ladies' man Eric Mendoza, has been seen—in the clinic!—with our newest patient, Hannah Bingham. Is this confirmed bachelor on his way to becoming an *instant* family man?

Chapter One

"Do I get a bonus if the buyer is young and pretty?" Jeanne asked.

Eric Mendoza tried to keep a stern expression, but it was nearly impossible when his fifty-something assistant arched her eyebrows and gave him an exaggerated wink.

"I think beautiful legs should play into the bonus equation, as well," she continued from her seat on the other side of his desk.

He held up a hand before she could detail what great breasts would be worth. "You'll get a bonus if the buyer is qualified. Looks and gender don't enter into it."

"Oh, sure, you say that now, but that's because you haven't *seen* the buyer."

Eric leaned back in his chair and sighed. "If I suggested your bonus would be based on anything else, you'd call me a sexist pig."

"Or worse," Jeanne agreed cheerfully. "I just love the double standard. I'm older and female, so I can say what I want. You're a young, good-looking executive on the rise, so you have to be careful."

"Right now I have to be busy." He pointed to the papers on his desk.

"Not a very subtle hint." Jeanne rose. "How long?"

He glanced at his computer screen. The schedule detailed there didn't leave much time for an unexpected meeting with a prospective purchaser of property twelve, but he wanted to get the house taken care of as quickly as possible.

"Ten minutes should be enough," he said.

"All right. I'll show her in and plan to interrupt in ten minutes." She grinned. "Should I knock before I enter, so I don't startle the two of you making out on the sofa?"

"I'm going to ignore that."

"Figures, but it wouldn't kill you to *think* about your social life from time to time. Once a quarter, at least. Eric, you need a woman."

"Jeanne, you need to stop trying to be my mother."

"Someone has to be. Besides, I'm good at it."

With that, she turned and headed out of the room. Eric watched her go.

His assistant was back talking, opinionated and invaluable. Through a quirk of fate, she'd been assigned to him after his first promotion three years before. Her smart mouth hid both superior intelligence and fierce loyalty. During his rapid rise to middle management at Merlyn County Regional Hospital, Jeanne had been a sounding board and a source of information. He was more than ten years younger than any of his peers, which created both resentment and opportunity. Jeanne kept a lot of the former at bay.

He scratched out a few more notes on his upcoming meeting, then glanced up when the door to his office opened.

"Hannah Wisham Bingham to see you," Jeanne said in her courteous "you're the boss" voice. Savvy as always, Jeanne only tortured him in private.

Eric set down his pen and rose. He was halfway across the room before both the name and the woman's appearance registered.

"Hannah?"

He studied the tall, slender blonde in his doorway, comparing her with the slightly gawky teenager he remembered from long-ago summers spent by the lake. Her eyes were still bright-green cat's eyes and her smile was familiar, but everything else had grown up…in the best way possible.

Her smile widened and a dimple appeared. "Eric. It's great to see you." She stepped into the room and glanced around. "Big office, a view. I'm impressed."

Behind Hannah's back, Jeanne gave him a thumb's-up of approval. He chuckled, then motioned to the sofa in the corner. "Hannah, please, have a seat."

When they were both settled and alone, he angled toward her. "This is a surprise. I didn't know you were back in town."

"I just got in a couple of days ago. I'm interested

in buying a house. I went through the various listings and was surprised to find one for sale by the hospital. Or is selling real estate something you do on the side?''

''I'm a man of many talents.''

''That's hardly news. So what's the scoop?''

She twisted her hand palm up as she spoke. Her long fingers moved gracefully. The tailored blazer and slim skirt she wore made her look like what she was now—a wealthy daughter of a socially prominent family. She'd come a long way from where she'd started.

''The hospital provides housing for visiting doctors and their families,'' he said. ''It's one way we attract the best and the brightest. The house up for sale is one of our properties. It's a great place, with views of the mountains and the lake, but it's a little too far out of town for doctors on call. I suggested we sell it and buy something closer to town. The board agreed with me.''

''I see. So you're in charge of getting rid of the old and buying the new, right?''

''I've already bought the new.''

''Why am I not surprised?'' She laughed. ''Off the beaten track with great views sounds like exactly what I'm looking for. When can I see it?''

''How about later this afternoon?''

''My calendar is blissfully free. Name the time.''

''Three.''

She tilted her head. Soft blond hair brushed across her shoulders. ''Will you be there, or do you delegate that sort of thing?''

''I'll be there,'' he told her, even as he knew it

would mean juggling an assortment of meetings and projects.

"Then we have a plan." She rose. "I'm looking forward to seeing the house and to talking with you more. We can catch up. It's been a long time."

He stood and smiled. "I agree. At least five years."

"Six." She shrugged. "Law school. It's teaching me to be precise."

She gave a little wave with her fingers, then headed for the door. Eric watched her go. Hannah had always been a pretty girl. Now she was a beautiful woman. No wonder Jeanne had wanted to know if there was a bonus for a buyer with great legs. Hannah had those in spades.

He returned to his desk. Less than ten seconds later, Jeanne burst in.

"Can I pick 'em or what?" she said, sounding pleased. "There's no husband—I asked."

He winced. "Typical."

Jeanne didn't bother looking chagrined. "I wanted to know. I knew *you* wouldn't ask..." Her gaze turned speculative. "Or would you already have this information at your fingertips? You two seemed to know each other."

"She's a couple of years younger than me. We met when we were teenagers. I worked at the lake, and she spent summers there. Her father is Billy Bingham."

Jeanne raised her eyebrows. "The younger, wilder son of the ever-so-wealthy Binghams? Didn't he die?"

"A long time ago."

About a year after Hannah had found out she was

his bastard daughter, Eric recalled. That had been the summer he and Hannah had met. Her grandmother had arranged for sailing lessons, and he'd been Hannah's instructor. He'd been all of sixteen, but had considered himself much older than her. Still, they'd become friends. Funny how Hannah had been the one person he could talk to back then.

"Now she's in town," Jeanne said. "I guess if she's a Bingham, we don't have to check her credit. She's bound to have money."

"I'm meeting her at the house at three. Please clear my afternoon."

Jeanne fluttered her eyelashes. "*You're* actually going to leave the office before seven-thirty in the evening?"

"Selling the house is my responsibility."

"Oh, don't feel you have to convince me you're doing the right thing. I'm all atwitter about this. I can't remember the last time you were on a date."

"My personal life—"

She cut him off with a shake of her head. "I know, I'm not supposed to say anything. I can't help it, Eric. Lord knows, practically every single woman between the ages of twenty and forty and living in a fifty-mile radius has tried to get your attention. But you ignore most of them. You only go out with the ones who aren't interested in anything but a good time. Don't you want to settle down and get married?"

He stared at her without responding.

She pressed her lips together. "Fine. Don't answer the question. Tell me it's none of my business and that you don't need me mothering you. But if you ask me, someone has to do it."

"I don't recall asking."

Jeanne didn't look the least bit discouraged. "I'm going back to my desk. I'll clear your afternoon. I know you think it's all about selling the house, but even you should notice that Hannah's a very attractive woman. You used to like her. Maybe you could again. Talk nice. Take her to dinner. It wouldn't kill you to get involved, you know."

With that, she left him alone.

Eric returned his attention to the report he'd been reading, but instead of seeing the sentences printed there, he considered Jeanne's words. That it wouldn't kill him to get involved with someone. She was right. It wouldn't.

But he'd learned a long time ago that it was far better to channel his energies into something concrete, like his career, than waste them trying to make a romantic relationship work. In his experience, women weren't likely to stick around, and love only led to tragedy.

But that didn't mean he couldn't enjoy the company of an old friend for an hour or two. And if she shared his philosophy of good times with no strings, then that hour or two could stretch into something longer.

While Hannah wouldn't mind holding on to a youthful complexion into her later years, she'd hoped that some parts of her *would* age. That maybe her veneer of sophistication would thicken into an actual part of her person. That she could be casually elegant in all situations. But no. Apparently you could take the girl out of Merlyn County, but you couldn't take Merlyn County out of the girl.

Laughing at herself, the beauty of the afternoon and the sense of having finally made the right choice, she steered her car up the two-lane road toward the house she wanted to see.

Spring had come to the area in an explosion of green leaves, budding flowers and a symphony of bird calls. She rolled down her window to inhale the sweetness in the air. After a cold winter in the close confines of university life in New Haven, she felt practically giddy at returning home.

She shifted in her seat. The truth had come to her somewhere in Virginia, as she'd driven back to Kentucky. She'd finally realized she wasn't so much running away from a life she didn't like as she was running *to* the one place where she'd always belonged. Unlike Dorothy who had only needed a pair of ruby slippers to find her way home, Hannah had required her faithful two-door coupe, several maps and nearly three days to make the journey. But she was here and she was about to make a fresh start.

Sort of. It seemed that time, distance and an Ivy League education had done little to help her get over her schoolgirl crush on Eric Mendoza. At fourteen, she'd thought he was the epitome of the cool, handsome older guy. Ten years later, he was all that and more—more successful, more polished, more filling out his well-cut suit.

At least she hadn't gushed. That was something. She would bet money he didn't have a clue as to how she'd felt all those years ago. She might have been madly in love with him, but she hadn't been an idiot.

She'd watched his string of girlfriends come and go. She'd been outclassed on the romantic playing field, but as his friend, she'd been the only female with staying power.

Now they were both grown-up. Equals, she told herself, then smiled. No, they weren't exactly equals. Not unless being around her made *his* heart thunder like a herd of elephants and his palms sweat. Given what she knew about him, she was going to guess the answer was no. Still, a girl could dream....

She glanced at her watch, then returned her attention to the winding road. Up ahead the street leveled out. On her left she saw a mailbox topped by the number she was looking for and pulled into the wide driveway. One curve later, she faced a wood and stone house with a pitched roof and views that seemed to stretch on forever.

Hannah slowed her car and sighed. She felt as if she'd just stepped into a Thomas Kinkade painting filled with lush colors and a mystical quality of light.

A stone wall fronted the house. There was a detached garage to the left and a gate to the right. From what she could see of the gardens, they were overgrown but still beautiful. Mature trees lined the property. A stone walk wound through the front yard, passing by two benches and what looked like a birdbath. There were plenty of windows, two narrow strips of stained glass on either side of the front door and several empty terra-cotta pots on the stone front porch.

Hannah parked her car next to a four-door BMW sedan and stepped out into the cool, sunny afternoon. She might only have seen the front of the house, but if the inside came close to matching, she was more than in love—she was ready to buy.

Eric walked around the side of the garage and approached her.

"What do you think?" he asked.

She tore her gaze away from the perfectly fitted eves and found herself caught up in his strong features and easy smile.

Time had chiseled his cheekbones into sharp relief and had added strength and stubbornness to his jaw. The hint of olive in his complexion made his teeth seem blindingly white, but, as always, it was his large dark eyes that captured her attention.

She remembered being fifteen, dealing with braces, bad skin and a growing crush on Eric. There had been countless nights spent in her room, writing awful poetry in an adolescent attempt to describe the wonder of his eyes. She'd never been able to find the words to detail the combination of browns and golds, nor had she been able to explain how his lashes could be so thick and long without being the least bit feminine.

Gorgeous house, gorgeous guy. What was a girl to do?

"It makes a great first impression," she said, motioning to the garden and walkway.

"Wait until you see inside. This property always received high marks from visiting doctors and their families."

He led the way to the gate and held it open. Hannah felt herself slipping back to adolescence when she noticed that even in two-inch heels, she was still several inches shorter than Eric. Talk about tall, dark and devastating.

One would think her relatively recent heartbreak would have taught her a thing or two about men with pretty faces, but one would be wrong. Apparently, handsome males from the past didn't count, or she hadn't learned her lesson.

Not wanting it to be the latter, she squared her shoulders and vowed that the rest of the afternoon would only be about business. She was interested in buying a house, Eric had one to sell—end of story.

While Eric pulled a key from his suit jacket pocket, Hannah stepped onto the small porch and glanced back at the garden. She could see how the hedges could be trimmed and the roses cut back. With a little TLC and a lot of weeding, the front garden could be a showpiece. She was going to have plenty of time and would welcome the exercise. Spending a few weeks out in the yard would be a great way to settle into coming home.

The front door opened and Eric stepped back to let her inside. The small foyer opened up into a large, empty living room complete with stone fireplace and arched windows. To the right of the entrance was the formal dining room, to the left was a hallway.

''How long has the house been vacant?'' she asked.

''About a month. Once we decided to sell the place, we waited for the family in residence to leave, then we painted it, inside and out.''

She glanced at the white walls. ''Great color choice.''

He chuckled. ''It's a little stark, but paint is easy to change.''

''Agreed.'' She already had a few ideas.

Hannah walked through to the kitchen, noting that

the hardwood floors flowed throughout the space. They were old, but in good shape, just like the cabinets and countertops. She wouldn't mind replacing the tile with granite, but that could easily wait. The appliances were new.

"How many bedrooms?" she asked.

"Two upstairs. Two more downstairs."

She frowned. "I thought this was a one-story."

"It looks that way from the street, but the house is built on the hillside and there's a daylight basement—family room, utility room and the additional two bedrooms."

She followed him into the living room and was able to see a staircase that led down.

Before exploring that part of the house, she walked into the two bedrooms on this floor. The master was large, with a modern and elegant bathroom and enough closet space for a beauty contestant. The second bedroom was smaller, but bright and sunny. Hannah paused, imagining what the room would look like with toys and child-size furniture.

The downstairs was as large and well lit as the upstairs. Only the utility and furnace rooms didn't have windows. There were the two extra bedrooms, another bathroom, a second fireplace and plenty of storage.

"I would have been happy with just the upstairs," she said as she rubbed her foot against the beige Berber carpet. "This is terrific."

Eric pulled open the sliding glass door in the family room and stepped outside. "Wait until you see this," he said with a grin.

She followed him outside. The backyard was huge

and level. A fence surrounded the property. Trimmed trees allowed a perfect view of the mountains, even from the ground level.

"Talk about a house with a view," Hannah murmured as she walked across the grass to the edge of the fence.

Eric paused by a wooden gate. "The house comes with a small boat dock."

"What?"

She stared down the side of the hill and saw stone steps leading to the lake below.

The sight of the blue water reminded her of happy afternoons spent on a sailboat. Ginman's Lake might not impress anyone who'd seen the Great Lakes or the ocean, but to the residents of the area it was paradise.

"Is this where I pretend disinterest, so you try to convince me it's perfect?" she asked, knowing that she'd found the place she wanted to call home.

Eric shook his head. "I'm not a salesman. I can tell you the price is fair, that I have maintenance records and receipts for the past seven years and that we'll pay for a five-year home warranty for all major systems and appliances."

She smiled. "Good to know. In return, I can tell you that I plan to pay cash."

He motioned back to the house. "Then let's go talk about it."

They walked through the house again and ended up sitting on the front steps. The sun warmed Hannah as she stretched out her legs and raised her face to the sky.

"I've missed this," she admitted. "All of it. Life here is a lot less complicated."

"It has its moments."

She turned to him. "I'm sure it does. You've been out of college—what, five years?—and you're already on the fast track."

"How would you know?"

"I could tell by the size of your office."

"Fair enough. I've worked hard and done well."

She remembered his plans to be rich and powerful. Growing up as somebody's bastard, on the wrong side of town, had a way of influencing a person's dreams. She knew from personal experience. The difference was while Eric had wanted success, she'd only wanted to belong.

"You're doing well yourself," he said. "Yale Law School. Congratulations."

"Thanks," she said, trying not to think about law school, or anything else related to her life in New Haven.

"This house will be a great summer place for you."

Hannah raised her eyebrows. "What?"

"Isn't that why you're buying it? So you'll have your own place when you come back in the summer?"

"No." She replayed their conversations and realized she'd never said why she was looking for a house. "This isn't going to be a vacation home for me. I'm moving back permanently."

Chapter Two

"Why?" Eric asked, sounding as disbelieving as he felt.

Hannah grinned. "Why would I give up life on the East Coast to return to Kentucky?"

"A good question for starters."

"I like it here." She glanced at him. "*You* didn't move away."

"Sure, but I found a good job here after college. If the right career choice had been in another city or state, I would have been gone."

"Hmm. Not me." She turned her attention back to the views. "I can tell you, there's no more beautiful place."

"You need to travel more."

She laughed. The soft, sweet sound made his chest tighten. His blood heated. It wasn't just her amusement, he acknowledged. It was the faintly floral scent of her skin, the clean lines of her profile, the slight arch in her eyebrows when she was amused.

"This is my home," she said.

"Of course." She was a Bingham, he reminded himself. Merlyn County meant family, roots and wealth.

"I'm not sure I liked the sound of that," she told him. "Why 'of course'?"

"You're one of them."

"Oh, please. A Bingham?" She wrinkled her nose. "I guess. I mean technically."

"Billy Bingham was your father. It doesn't get more technical than that."

"For what it's worth, I don't feel like a 'them.' I'm still that girl who grew up poor. A really cool night in my house was fast food and a movie."

"Now it's French champagne."

She laughed again. "Will you think less of me if I confess I've never actually had French champagne?"

"I wouldn't believe you."

"It's true. I'm not much of a drinker to begin with and most of the parties I attended at college were more beerfests than high-society get-togethers. I certainly never drink around the Binghams. I'd be too scared to put a foot wrong."

"Yet you want to move next door."

"Good point." She frowned slightly. "This isn't exactly next door. They're on the other side of town."

Not much distance around here, he thought humorously, but he wasn't going to remind her.

"I can't believe you didn't want to settle in Paris," he said instead.

She raised her eyebrows. "Trust me. There's not *that* much money. Although moving over there would solve the champagne problem, huh?"

"I've heard they drink it for breakfast."

Her eyes widened. "On their cereal?"

"With a baguette and cheese."

Her nose wrinkled again. "No, thanks. I'll stick with a bagel and fruit, even if that means doing without the champagne."

"Probably a good choice."

"I'm a country girl at heart."

He eyed her well-cut clothing. "You don't look like a country girl."

She fingered her skirt, then lowered her voice. "Outlet store. You would die if you knew how little I paid for it."

"I doubt that."

She chuckled. "Okay, so you don't have the shopping thing going on. I might be a Bingham now, but I still know how to stretch a dollar until it screams for mercy."

Something she would have learned from her mother, he reminded himself.

"Is your sister still in town?" she asked.

"Sure. CeCe works at the Women's Health Center. She's a midwife."

Hannah nodded. "I think I remember knowing that before. She must really love her work."

"She does."

"And you?" She tilted her head. "Enjoying clawing your way up the corporate ladder?"

"Every inch of it."

"I'm not sure I would," she admitted humorously.

"But my uncle Ron is unlikely to invite me into the boardroom, so it's not a problem."

Ronald Bingham, CEO of Bingham Enterprises, was known as a man skilled at business. Eric had met him at a few charity events and had been impressed. Ron didn't seem to be the kind of executive who granted family members special favors.

"You might have to start in the mail room," he teased.

"I have no doubt. Which is why I won't be applying." She turned toward him. "Hey, wait a minute. First you tell me I could live anywhere, and now you're telling me my uncle won't give me a really cool job, despite my lack of experience. I'm starting to take this personally. You don't want me moving back here, do you?"

He held up both hands in a gesture of surrender. "I never said that. I'm delighted you're back."

"Really?"

"Sure."

Her green eyes darkened slightly, and her mouth relaxed. Eric found himself studying her face as the humor faded, leaving subtle tension in its wake.

Sexual tension, he acknowledged. The air was thick with it, right under the jokes and teasing. His fingers itched to stroke the curve of her cheek, while for points farther south he had something more erotic in mind.

It was rare for a woman to get his attention during the workday. In fact, it had been several months since one had captured his eye at all. Why Hannah? Why now?

Was it the appeal of the grown-up version of someone he'd always liked? That, combined with her intelligence, quick wit and beauty, made her a difficult woman to resist. Maybe he didn't want to resist her. Maybe giving in would feel pretty damned good.

"What are you thinking?" she asked softly.

"You don't want to know."

"Maybe I do."

"I was thinking you're all grown up," he admitted. "You've finished college and law school and now you're..."

He frowned as he quickly did the math. Hannah was a couple of years younger than him, which meant if she'd taken the usual four years to get through college, she shouldn't have had time to complete her law degree.

"When did you graduate?" he asked.

"From law school?"

He nodded.

She sighed. "I haven't yet." She held up a hand. "I know, I know. You're dying to give me some kind of lecture. Believe me, I heard it in spades from my professors. I needed a break, so I left and came home." She stared past him. "There were things I needed to figure out."

He had questions, but he held them back. She might be an old friend, but he didn't have the right to grill her about her decisions. Even if they didn't make sense to him. Walk away from an Ivy League law degree? Not even on a bet.

"Okay, I'm changing the subject," she said with a smile. "Assuming I want to buy the house, which I do, what's the next step?"

"I have all the paperwork and disclosures at the

office. I can get them to you. After you review everything, you make an offer. It will be contingent on credit approval—which, in your case, means confirming you have the money—and a building inspection. Once that's done we could close in a matter of a week or so."

"Wow. That's fast. I could be in before the end of the month?"

"Sure. If that's what you'd prefer."

"It is. I'm staying at the Lakeshore Inn, which is nice, but not home."

"What about your place in New Haven?"

She shrugged. "It was a small grad student apartment. We're talking zero room and tiny windows. Trust me, I won't miss it." She waved at the yard. "Not when I get a beautiful house and all this. I'm dying to tidy up the garden."

He glanced at the overrun plants and birdbath. His concept of horticulture ended with the knowledge that lawns had to be cut when they got too long.

"What are you going to do?" he asked, both curious and interested in prolonging the conversation. Eventually he was going to have to get back to the office, but not just yet. Talking with Hannah would be worth working later than usual.

"The whole front yard needs some serious tidying," she said eagerly. "Can you imagine what this place must be like in summer? With the climbing roses in bloom and the flowers everywhere? I want to weed the path and clean out the birdbath." She pointed to the left. "And on the side of the house I'm going to plant berries."

He stared at her. "Berries?"

"Uh-huh. Strawberries and blueberries and raspberries. They won't all produce fruit this year, but next year I'll have a great harvest."

"Berries?"

"Why do you keep saying that? Don't you like berries?"

"Sure, but—"

She rolled her eyes. "Let me guess. Not enough to plant them. You probably buy them at the grocery store."

"Sometimes."

"Figures. You could grow them fresh, you know."

"I live in a condo with a patio. There's not much room."

"Okay, well, *I* can grow them, and I really want to. When I was with my mom we had raspberries and blueberries. I would eat them all summer. She would freeze some and sometimes we'd make ice cream."

"That all sounds really great," he said as he tried to keep from smiling.

Her eyes narrowed. "Mock me all you want, big guy, but come next summer you're going to be begging for blueberries and I'll just turn my back on you."

"You'd never be that mean."

"Probably not, but I'll verbally abuse you before handing them over."

He chuckled. "Hannah, you've grown up into an amazing woman."

"Thank you. You're not so bad yourself."

He'd meant the comment to be both teasing and a compliment. He suspected she'd responded in kind. But he doubted either of them had planned to send the tension level soaring. Awareness crackled between them, making the hairs on the back of his neck stand up. He could feel the heat growing, along with a very specific need.

Was she aware of it, as well, or was he feeling this all on his own? There was only one way to find out.

"Would you have dinner with me tomorrow?" he asked. "Unless there's a Mr. Hannah waiting in the wings."

"There's no one." She tucked her hair behind her ears. "I'd like to have dinner with you."

"It's a date."

Her eyes widened slightly. "That's definitive."

"Would you prefer we just go as friends?"

She swallowed. "No. A date is nice. I've never been on a date in Kentucky."

"Really? Then I'll have to get you a copy of the handbook. You don't want to break any important rules your first time out."

"Certainly not. People would talk."

"They're going to talk anyway."

She smiled. "It seems to be a universal hobby."

"So I'll pick you up at your hotel. Lakeshore Inn, right?"

She nodded. "Room fourteen. What time?"

"Seven work?"

"Sure."

He glanced at his watch. "I've really enjoyed this, but if you could see my desk."

"I know. You're busy. It's the corporate shark in you." She pointed to the door. "Would you mind leaving that open so I can look around a little more? I'll lock it when I'm done."

"I'll do you one better." He handed her the key. "You can return that to me tomorrow."

"Are you sure?"

"Yeah. I trust you not to spray paint the walls or run off with the appliances."

She laughed. "I don't think I could physically carry the refrigerator. But I would appreciate the chance to come back with a tape measure and start making plans."

"Help yourself. In the meantime I'll get the paperwork pulled together. Someone will bring the information on the house by in the morning."

"Such service." She stood. "I'm impressed."

So was he, he thought as he rose, but for different reasons.

He hesitated for a second. The urge to lean forward and kiss her was strong. More than strong. He had a feeling she might not object. But this was a business meeting, unlike their dinner, which would be purely pleasure.

"I'll see you tomorrow," he said.

"I'm looking forward to it."

He waved and headed for his car. Anticipation filled him. He had it bad, and, boy, did that feel good.

The home improvement store on the edge of town was a recent addition to the area. Hannah pushed her oversize cart down the wide aisles and figured a person could get lost in here and not be seen for years. She'd already had to ask twice to find her way back to the window coverings. Now she stared at an assortment of miniblinds that boggled her mind.

"And I thought the fabric store was confusing,"

she murmured to herself as she took in the different colors and textures available.

Her first priority was to decorate the upstairs. That's where she would be living. Eventually she would find uses for the rooms downstairs, but there was no rush. Still, during her second, slower walk-through the previous afternoon, she'd noticed that neither of the downstairs bedroom windows had coverings. She wanted something up before she moved in.

She fingered the plastic blinds, then the metal. There were also wooden blinds, but she wasn't sure she wanted to make that much of a financial investment.

"I could always tack up sheets," she reminded herself. It might be an easier and cheaper solution.

Oh, but it felt good to have this kind of decision to make, she thought happily. While she'd barely read over the sales contracts Eric had sent over, she felt a sense of ownership toward the house. It was everything she'd ever wanted in a home.

It was also the first real home she'd known since she was thirteen and her mother had died. Before then, she'd happily lived in the old, dilapidated two-bedroom shack. Sure it had been drafty and cramped, but she'd never known anything else. After her mother's death, she'd spent a few confusing weeks at the Bingham mansion, living with her grandmother and meeting her father for the first time. Mourning her mother's loss while dealing with a family she'd never known had been too much for her to handle. She'd been grateful when the decision had been made to send her off to an all-girls' boarding school.

Since then she'd lived in dorms and more recently

in a small apartment. But those had all been temporary places. For the first time in just over ten years she was going to have a place of her own, and that felt really good.

She abandoned the miniblind confusion and headed for the gardening section. Maybe someone there could tell her if it was too late to plant berries. She smiled as she pictured the profusion of vines and leaves and bright, ripe berries. Her mother had always frozen several quarts and turned others into jam. Hannah wasn't sure she remembered much more than the basics, but she could probably find a recipe somewhere.

Oh my, she thought with a chuckle. Whatever would her friends from college and law school think of her now if they knew she was excited by the idea of shopping for window coverings and making her own jam. They wouldn't even recognize her.

She slowed as she approached the garden center. In some ways she didn't recognize herself. For the first time in her life she wasn't going along with what everyone else wanted and expected. She was doing what was right for her.

She entered the large, covered area next to the main building and inhaled the scent of plants. A sign overhead pointed her in the direction of the berries, but before she could head that way, she heard someone call her name.

''Hannah?''

She turned and saw a tall, handsome man walking toward her. Hannah was two parts pleased, one part chagrined. In a town this small, she'd known that running into a member of her extended family was inevitable, but she hadn't thought it would happen so soon.

Ronald Bingham, powerful, successful and charming, ran Bingham Enterprises with the ease of someone born to power. As he had been. Technically he was her uncle—her late father's brother—but as she'd never grown up around him, she simply thought of him as the slightly scary, very kind, head of the family.

"It *is* you," he said as he approached.

She smiled. "You caught me lurking in the garden section of the home improvement store. Whatever will Grandmother say?"

She spoke lightly to cover her suddenly fluttering nerves.

"I have no idea," Ron said as he hugged her, then kissed her cheek. "Probably that you look lovely." He held her at arm's length. "Whatever you've been doing agrees with you, Hannah."

"Thank you." She hoped he would still think that when she answered the inevitable questions, then braced herself for a barrage when he dived right in.

"Shouldn't you be in New Haven?" he asked. "Is this a school holiday?"

"I should be at Yale and yet I'm not," she told him. "I'm here instead."

"Want to tell me why?"

She studied his strong face and hazel eyes. She'd shown up in his family with little warning. Yet another of Billy Bingham's bastards. Ron had only ever been kind and welcoming. She hoped that wouldn't change.

"Would you be okay if I told you no and made a feeble attempt to change the subject?" she asked.

"I think I'd survive."

"Good." She smiled. "So what are you doing hanging out here with the plants? Don't you have an empire to run?"

He laughed. "Sure, but sometimes there are too many meetings. That's when I duck out for a couple of hours. I'm putting a new deck on the house and I thought I'd come by and check out the lumber."

"Don't you have flunkies and contractors to do that for you?"

"Of course, but if they did, I couldn't tell my assistant that I needed to do it myself and get away."

"Couldn't you just take a day off?"

He glanced around as if checking to make sure they were alone, then lowered his voice. "A day off isn't as much fun as sneaking away for a couple of hours."

"The thrill of cutting classes?"

"Something like that."

"And here I thought you always followed the rules."

"Not when it suits me to break them."

"Good to know." She leaned against her cart. "Still, looking at lumber isn't much of an excuse."

"I don't need a better one. I'm the boss. So what are you doing back in town?"

She sighed. "Didn't I just duck that question?"

"Only temporarily. Sorry, Hannah, I'm going to keep after you until I know everything is all right."

She wanted to tell him that he didn't have to worry about her but doubted he would listen. Even though she hadn't spent much time around the Binghams she knew Ron considered her family. In a way his concern felt nice. Unfortunately, his disappointment was going to make her squirm.

"I've moved back to town."

His steady gaze never wavered. "What about law school?"

"I still have about eighteen months left."

He studied her for a couple of seconds before speaking. "No one knows, right?"

She nodded.

"And you don't want anyone to know."

"Not exactly." Not yet. In time, word would get out, but Hannah was hoping for later rather than sooner. "I know my window for keeping a secret is limited."

"Especially around here." He touched her shoulder. "All right, kid. I won't say a word. Not even to Myrtle."

"Thanks," Hannah said, trying not to wince at the mention of her grandmother. The matriarch of the family wouldn't take the news of Hannah's decision nearly as well as Ron had.

"Are you all right?" he asked. "Anything I can help you with?"

"I'm fine," she promised. "Oh, but I do need the name of a real estate lawyer. I'm buying a house."

He raised his eyebrows. "You weren't kidding about moving back."

"Not even for a second."

"All right. Let me get the name and number of a good real estate lawyer. I have the information back at the office. Where are you staying?"

"The Lakeshore Inn."

"I'll leave you a message."

"I appreciate that. Really."

"My pleasure." He glanced at his watch. "I have to head back to the office. You take care, Hannah. If you need anything, you know how to get in touch with me."

"I do. Thank you again. For everything."

She hugged him, then waved as he walked out of the store. She knew that when she returned to the hotel he would have already left a message for her. He was that sort of man—kind, dependable, thoughtful.

And lonely. He didn't show it as much as he had a couple of years ago, but she could see it in his eyes. Violet, his late wife, had been gone for years, and still Ron mourned her. Her unexpected death had stunned everyone, but him most of all. They'd been in love until the day she'd died.

At least, that's what Hannah had always heard. She'd only experienced the couple together firsthand a couple of times before Violet died. But Hannah had seen Ron suffering as he struggled to go on and raise his kids without their mother.

While Hannah was pleased to see that he'd gotten better, she couldn't help envying the love he and Violet had shared. What would it be like to love and be loved that much? To be first in someone's life? It was the one thing she'd always wanted. Would it ever happen? Could she ever be first in someone's life?

There was no answer to that question waiting in the plant department, nor was she likely to find one anywhere today. Better to focus on her errands and the house and things she could control. Like what she was going to say to her grandmother when Myrtle found out Hannah had moved back for good. It wasn't a conversation she eagerly anticipated.

Unfortunately, her move wasn't the only secret she kept. Pausing in the aisle, Hannah pressed her hand against her barely bulging stomach. True to form with a first pregnancy, she was barely showing at all—even being nearly four months along.

If her grandmother was going to hit the roof over Hannah moving back, imagine what the older woman would say when she found out there was a grandchild on the way…and no father to be seen.

"Maybe we could make a video of the conversation and sell it to Hollywood," she murmured as she walked down the aisles of plants. "More reality TV."

Her grandmother wasn't the only one who was going to be surprised. Hannah didn't want to think about Eric's reaction to the news that she was pregnant. Of course what with him not being the father, it wasn't actually his business. Still, she knew that if they continued to see each other, she was going to have to come clean at some point or risk him thinking she had a serious problem with excessive bloat.

But she didn't have to tell him anytime soon. One dinner did not a relationship make.

Chapter Three

Spurred on by the reward of dinner with Hannah, Eric had left work on time for once. After heading home for a quick shower and change of clothes, he showed up at her hotel exactly on time. She opened the door and smiled.

"Eric."

He'd heard his name spoken hundreds of time, even by Hannah. But there was something about the way she said it tonight. Sort of breathlessly, as if she'd thought about seeing him and had enjoyed the anticipation.

He didn't usually allow himself to be distracted during his workday, but this afternoon had been an exception. More than once his thoughts had strayed to tonight. Seeing her now, he knew he hadn't underestimated her allure.

She wore her blond hair loose and curled. Makeup accentuated her big, green eyes. A soft peach-colored dress dipped low enough to heat his blood while falling to just above her knees.

She was older, more sophisticated and five kinds of temptation. He was a man who hadn't been tempted in a while. He liked the odds.

"Official legal documents," he said as he handed over the contracts.

"Oh, good. I have the name of a real estate lawyer. I'm going to run these over to her in the morning."

She took the folder and set it on the desk by the door, then offered him the house key. "Everything is exactly as we left it."

"I'm not worried."

"Good."

She collected her purse and stepped into the hallway. "Where to?"

He laughed. "You ask that as if there are a dozen choices. This isn't New York."

"Really?" She feigned surprise. "That explains the lack of traffic noise. I wondered why it was so quiet."

They took the stairs to the main floor.

"So what did you do today?" he asked as they crossed the lobby. "Buy any berry plants?"

She glanced at him. "You mock me now, but you'll be the one crawling down my garden path, begging for a sample."

Eric didn't doubt there could be begging involved, but it wouldn't be for fruit.

They stepped out into the early evening. The sun

had set, leaving a trail of pink along the western horizon. A few stars were already visible.

Hannah drew in a deep breath. ''I've missed being here,'' she said. ''It's good to be back.''

''Wait until the summer humidity kicks in.''

She shook her head. ''It's not going to bother me. I plan to enjoy every sweaty second.''

''If it gets too bad, you can go float in the lake.''

''That's true. It will only be a few short steps away.''

He reached in his slacks pocket for his car keys and hit the remote. The dark-blue BMW 330i unlocked. He opened the passenger door.

''Nice car.''

''Yeah.'' He grinned. ''I know. It's an indulgence. I've always had a thing for cars, but I was too busy putting food on the table or working my way through school to have one that wasn't basic transportation. When I got my last promotion, I figured it was time.''

She touched his arm. ''You've more than earned it. I'm just glad you're able to enjoy your success. Some people seem to get so caught up in getting more and more that they forget to enjoy what they have.''

She slid onto the passenger seat. He closed the door and walked around to the driver's side.

The BMW had been his first and only indulgence. He lived simply and put most of his money in the bank. But getting the car had fulfilled a dream he'd had since he'd been a kid and had seen the rich folks in town driving their fancy cars. He didn't care about big houses or snazzy vacations, but a car was something different.

A guy thing, his sister, CeCe, would tell him. She'd

never understood his fascination with horsepower and body style and had never once been willing to discuss the importance of letting an engine breathe correctly.

At sixteen, saving to buy a car had been as important as saving for college. While he didn't regret those days, he was glad they were behind him. His hard work had paid off. He had a good career and a great life and was about to have dinner with a beautiful woman.

"You never told me what you did today," he said. "Did you go to the house again?"

"Of course. I love it more each time I see it. I did some measuring for miniblinds downstairs and tried to figure out what would go where in the upstairs rooms. Then I visited a couple of furniture places and the home improvement store. I could spend a fortune there."

"That would make you popular."

They arrived at Melinda's, one of the few upscale restaurants in town. Eric parked and came around to open Hannah's door.

"What do you think?" he asked as he pointed at the converted firehouse. "It hasn't changed much."

Hannah glanced around. "I never came here very often. It's not exactly a hangout for the college crowd. My grandmother brought me before I left for law school and I remember it being very nice."

They walked in, and the hostess took them upstairs to a table. When they were seated, Eric fingered the wine list.

"Can I interest you?" he asked.

She shook her head. "No, thanks."

"Too bad. You're messing with my plans."

She raised her eyebrows. ''Ha. Let me guess. You wanted to ply me with alcohol and then take advantage of my weakened condition.''

That hadn't been his plan, but hers had some appeal. ''Any chance it would work?''

She gave him a haughty look. ''I assure you, I'm not that kind of girl.''

No surprise. He leaned toward her. ''What kind are you?''

''Right now, one in transition. Ask me in a couple of months. I'll have a better answer.''

''Rethinking your idea to move back?''

''No.'' She touched her menu. ''That feels right.''

He pushed away the wine list. ''I wasn't really thinking about getting you drunk.''

''I know.'' She looked at him from under her lashes. ''You were never one of those guys who needed tricks to get what he wanted from a woman.''

Eric raised a hand, palm toward her. ''Wait a minute. How would you know?''

''I heard things. And saw them.''

''What things?''

''All those girls hanging around when you were working down by the lake. You were the most popular sailing instructor there.''

Eric shrugged off her comments. ''That was a long time ago.''

''Uh-huh, and so much has changed? Are you telling me you ever struggle to get a date?''

He didn't want to talk about his social life. Not only did he not have one, for the most part he wasn't interested. He had his career to worry about.

''Enough about me. How many broken hearts are you leaving in New Haven?'' he asked.

''Practically none.''

The waiter appeared before she could say more. He detailed the specials of the evening and took their drink orders. Hannah asked for club soda while Eric chose Scotch.

When the waiter left, Hannah opened her menu.

''It was interesting driving around town today,'' she said. ''I can see a few changes. But Merlyn County is fundamentally the same.''

''Does that make it seem more like home?''

She considered the question. ''Yes. I know when I left for the first time, I was pretty shocked by the outside world. I'd never even been beyond the county line, and there I was, getting on a plane.''

Back then Eric would have considered leaving town an adventure, but he doubted it had been that way for Hannah. Her mother had died at the beginning of the summer and by the end, Hannah had left.

''Were you scared?''

''Terrified,'' she admitted with a smile. ''Of course I'd never been to a boarding school. I'd barely read about them in books. I didn't fit in with the girls there at all.'' She wrinkled her nose. ''Most of them had never met anyone born west of Philadelphia. One girl actually asked me if I ate 'possum.''

''They're serving 'possum fajitas down at the Mexican stand,'' he teased.

She rolled her eyes. ''They wouldn't have been surprised by that, believe me. But it wasn't all bad. I made friends and started to fit in. I never could find pure joy in reading fashion magazines but we had other things in common.''

''And you got to see something of the world.''

''Right. An all-girls' boarding school in the middle of nowhere. Call me a world traveler.'' She shook her head. ''There wasn't even a boys' school nearby. Instead, all three hundred of us had to fight over the five teenage guys who lived in the small town next to the school. It was horrible. I didn't have my first date until college.''

He frowned. ''What about when you came back here for the summer? I remember you hanging out with a lot of guys.''

''You remember me hanging out with large groups.''

''No one asked you out?''

''I appreciate how incredulous you sound, but the answer is still no. I guess no one was brave enough to face my grandmother when he came to pick me up.''

''So I should be grateful you're staying at a hotel?''

''It depends. Does Myrtle Bingham terrify you as much as she terrifies me?''

''At eighteen I would have been shaking in my boots. I'm pretty sure I could handle her now.''

''Great. Then you can be the one to tell her I've made a permanent move back. I haven't worked up the courage yet.''

That surprised him. ''She doesn't know?''

''Not yet. But I saw Uncle Ron today, so word is slowly spreading.''

The waiter appeared with the drinks. After looking over the menu, Eric and Hannah ordered.

When the waiter left, she swirled her straw around in her glass. "I didn't mean to make my years at boarding school sound awful. I received a terrific education. And there were a lot of fun times. A friend and I found a baby raccoon once and raised it. Of course when it got too big, it completely destroyed our room, but it was worth it. And we had a lot of wonderful visiting professors. They would come for one term and teach us interesting things like architecture or philosophy. There was one who came from England and did a series of seminars on British royalty."

She sipped her drink. "He had a teenage son with him. Very cute. All the girls went crazy over him."

Eric remembered Hannah's youthful clean-scrubbed good looks and long blond hair. "Why didn't *you* go out with him?"

She gave him a pitying glance. "For one thing, he never asked. For another, he didn't actually date, although he did sleep with a lot of girls. It was quite the scandal. Still, I can recite the entire royal lineage from the War of the Roses to the present day."

"Impressive."

"Want me to prove it?"

"No."

She laughed. "Fair enough. So enough about my past. What about yours? You were always a heart-throb when you worked at the lake. All those young women fluttering around you...the tiny bikinis, the suntan lotion they couldn't seem to apply themselves."

"I had dates."

"I remember. Dozens."

Eric shrugged. "When I wasn't working, I was playing." The free time had been infrequent, and he'd taken advantage of it. If the local girls had wanted to share it with him, who was he to object?

But he'd never gone out with Hannah. For one thing, she'd been a couple of years younger. That didn't seem like much now, but back then it had been a big difference. For another, they'd been friends. Her grandmother had paid for her to take sailing lessons, and he'd been her teacher.

She'd been different from the other girls. Quieter. More sensible. She hadn't talked about clothes or boys. He'd found himself able to open up to her. Aside from his sister, Hannah had been the only person he'd ever told about his dreams to go to college and make something of himself. She hadn't laughed.

"You were a good friend," he said.

"Thank you. You were, too. You listened to me complain about not fitting in with the Binghams and how I hated leaving every summer."

He remembered. "You told me who thought I was cute."

"Yeah, like you needed help in that department." She met his gaze. "Now we're both grown up."

Five simple words that shouldn't have meant anything, he told himself. Yet they created an awareness that crackled like spring lightning. Or was he imagining the heat between them?

There was only one way to find out. But did he want to risk taking things to the next level before learning if Hannah was a member of the "as long as it feels good" club? After all, she'd always been a good girl. Was that likely to have changed?

Probably not, he told himself, but a guy could dream. And Hannah was exactly the kind of fantasy he liked to have.

"Tell me about your work at the hospital," she suggested as the waiter arrived with their salads. "The name plate on your door said you were a director. That has to be a big deal."

"It's a recent promotion."

"How far do you plan to move up the food chain?"

"Right to the top."

"And when you get there?"

"I'll find another challenge."

She picked up her fork. "Great. And my big excitement for the day was choosing miniblinds. Which I was unable to do. Too much selection."

"Hi, Eric, sorry to interrupt."

Eric looked up and saw Mari Bingham pause by the table. The attractive brunette smiled sheepishly.

"I know, I know, this isn't the place to discuss business, but I was hoping I could—"

She broke off when she glanced at his companion. Her hazel eyes widened in surprise. "Hannah?"

"Hi, Mari. How's it going?"

Mari's smiled broadened. "What are you doing here? I thought you were still in law school back East. Grandmother didn't say anything about you being in town."

"I know," Hannah said, hedging. "You look great. How are things?"

"Good. Busy, of course. There are always fifty million directions I could go in at any one time."

As Mari continued speaking, Eric glanced between the two women. They were friendly enough, but there was a lack of closeness. In this case, he guessed the cause was Hannah's relatively late discovery of her relationship with the Binghams. She and Mari might be cousins, but they hadn't grown up together.

"So when did you get into town?" Mari asked.

"Few days ago."

Mari looked poised to keep on with the questions, and Eric had a feeling Hannah would prefer to avoid them for the time being.

"What work did you want to discuss?" he asked.

Mari turned to him. "Oh, right. I'm interrupting."

"Not at all."

She grinned. "Good looks and perfect manners. You're still a heartbreaker, Eric."

He chuckled. "Sure. I leave a trail of tragic women everywhere I go. So why are you pouring on the compliments?"

"I need your help."

He motioned to an extra chair. "Please, have a seat."

"No, thanks. I don't want to take up too much of your time." She glanced over her shoulder, then back at him. When she spoke, her voice was lower.

"I need your help with funding, for a new research facility."

That surprised him. "Hardly my area of expertise."

"Don't panic. I don't need you to raise the money. I just want you onboard with my plan. If you're in agreement, then senior management will be more open to it."

"I appreciate the vote of confidence, Mari, but I'm only a director."

"One on the fast track. I hear things. So can we set up a meeting?"

"Sure. Give me a call in the morning and we'll arrange something."

Mari thanked him. "You're the best," she said, then glanced at Hannah. "Enjoy your dinner with our local heartthrob."

Hannah laughed. "I promise."

"Let's have lunch or something soon," Mari suggested.

"That would be great."

Mari waved and left them alone.

Eric turned back to Hannah only to find her grinning at him.

He shook his head. "Don't go there."

"Where?" she asked innocently.

"Wherever you were planning to go."

"I'm staying right here." She stabbed a piece of lettuce. "It's not every day that a girl like me gets lucky enough to have dinner with someone so famous."

He groaned. "Hannah, you're going there."

She batted her eyelashes. "Someone on the management fast track and a real heartbreaker. And me just a poor country girl. I'm not even sure how to keep from embarrassing myself." She leaned close. "Am I using the right fork and all?"

He picked up his drink. "I'm ignoring you."

"All right. I'm finished." She sighed. "But it's comforting to know that some things never change. You were a hit with the ladies before and you still are. I like the consistency."

He shrugged. It was true that dating had always

been pretty easy for him. More women said yes than no, but in the end, what did it matter? He was looking for a good time, nothing more. He'd long ago learned that love didn't last, and when it ended, people left.

"You sounded surprised that Mari wanted your help," she said.

"She's never asked for it before. I don't know what she thinks I can do, but I'm willing to get onboard."

"She works hard."

"It's a family trait."

Hannah set down her fork. "I agree. Which is why I hadn't mentioned my return home to her or anyone." She glanced at him, then away. "You probably noticed she didn't know."

He nodded. "It's your decision, Hannah."

"I know. I tell myself that, but there's still plenty of guilt to go around."

He didn't know about her guilt, but he was willing to admit he thought she was crazy to give up an Ivy League law degree to return to Merlyn County. Still, it was her choice.

"If Mari *and* my Uncle Ron know I'm back in town," she said, "I guess it's not going to stay a secret very long."

"Did you expect it to?"

"No. But I'd sort of hoped."

"That no one would notice you'd returned?"

"Silly, huh?"

She spoke softly, as if afraid of being judged. Eric wanted to reach across the table and take her hand in his while reassuring her that he was nothing but pleased she was back.

"Not silly," he told her.

"But not completely logical."

"Do you want to be logical?" he asked.

"Don't you think it's a good characteristic for a lawyer?"

"It would help."

"Then I guess I'll have to work on it."

"Are you planning to go back to law school?"

She briefly closed her eyes. "I'm wildly confused about my life. Let's talk about you instead. Tell me everything you do in a day."

"I have meetings."

"And?"

He shrugged. "I write reports. I check on how other people are doing. You know, management stuff."

She smiled. "Stuff? You're a recently promoted director at a major hospital and you refer to your work as stuff?"

He laughed. "Yes. Ask Jeanne. There's plenty of stuff to go around."

She leaned forward. "You don't actually do work, do you? It's all a facade."

"You've discovered my secret."

Her green eyes widened. "Is that the only one?"

He thought about how appealing he found her. "Not even close."

"Oh, good. I'm going to have to pry them all out of you. What would be my best course of action?"

"You want me to tell you how to discover my secrets? Shouldn't you be the one figuring that out?"

"I could, but it would be so much easier if you simply confessed all. So…how can I make you confess?"

He could think of a half-dozen ways, but none of them could take place in a very public restaurant.

"I'm not telling."

"Fine. Then I'll just have to guess."

Hannah found herself enjoying dinner more than she would have thought. Her crush on Eric aside, she found him easy to talk to, easy to look at and plenty funny. There hadn't been any awkward moments, not even when her cousin Mari had appeared unexpectedly. If Eric thought she was a fool for trying to keep her presence in town a secret, he was polite enough not to say anything.

She liked how he was obviously capable and successful but didn't feel the need to brag about his accomplishments. Over the years she'd heard plenty of guys willing to detail exactly how wonderful they were and why she should be impressed just by breathing the same air. Eric let his actions speak for him.

Now, seated in his car as they drove back to her hotel, she faced the age-old dilemma that had haunted women since they were first picked up by Ug at the edge of the cave. Where, exactly, were they going to say good-night and what was going to happen when they did?

As she had a small suite rather than just a room, she could invite Eric upstairs without making it seem as if she had the wild thing on her mind. Not that she didn't find him attractive and sexy. She did. In spades. But it was a first date and there was the whole matter of her pregnancy. She didn't show in clothes yet, but naked, there was an obvious tummy.

Yikes! She shook her head and forced images of a naked Eric out of her mind. This was a *first* date. She never did much more than offer a quick peck on the cheek on a first date. Sex was out of the question. He didn't want to, as far as she knew, and she didn't want to, either. Well, she wasn't going to act on what she might find interesting to think about, that was for sure.

"I had a good time," Eric said, rescuing her from the whirlwind of her mind.

"Me, too."

"Want to do it again sometime?"

"Sure," she said, knowing it was the truth, even if seeing him didn't fit into her plan of moving home to make her life less complicated.

They pulled into the parking lot of her hotel. Hannah sucked in a breath. Okay. Decision time. What to say, what to do? At some point, if they continued to see each other, she was going to have to tell him about the baby. Right now it was a nonissue. No way was she going to get into it in the middle of a parking lot. If things progressed, there would be plenty of time for that. As for asking him up…

He pulled into a space and turned off the engine. After unhooking his seat belt, he turned toward her and took her hand.

"I plan to walk you to your room," he said, his voice low and sexy enough to make her shiver. "But the hallway is pretty public for a good-night kiss."

Kiss? They were going to kiss? Hannah was both delighted and terrified. The last guy she'd kissed had been a complete disaster. But Eric was different. And she wanted to kiss him. A lot.

He leaned toward her. She found herself responding by releasing her seat belt and inching toward his side. They met somewhere in the middle.

It was just a kiss, she told herself, the second before his mouth settled on hers. It didn't mean anything.

But as his warm, firm lips touched her own, she found herself wishing it could at least mean a little something. Or maybe even a lot.

Chapter Four

Eric kissed like a man who enjoyed the activity for its own sake and not just as a pit stop on the road to victory. Hannah enjoyed the feel of his mouth, the weight of his hand on her shoulder, the feel of his body so close to hers. There was plenty of heat flaring between them and lots of enticingly melty sensations in her midsection and just a tad lower. She felt tingly and squirmy and more than a little aroused.

All this and the kiss was still chaste. What on earth was going to happen if things progressed even a little?

At the thought of even more exciting sensations, her brain overloaded and shut down. Which was fine. It meant she could concentrate on the brush of lips against lips and on the pleasingly masculine scent of his skin and the softness of his freshly shaven cheeks.

He brushed his mouth back and forth against hers

before settling into place. There was just the right amount of pressure—enough to show interest without trying to overwhelm. When he moved his hand so he cupped the back of her head, she leaned in even closer. At the same moment he brushed her lower lip with his tongue.

The warm, damp stroke made her shiver. The summer she'd turned sixteen, and the two summers following, she'd spent more time than she could ever admit wondering what it would be like to be kissed by Eric. She was just rational enough to be grateful the experience was even better than she'd imagined. As she parted her mouth, she braced herself for the impact of his tongue against hers. Of wet seeking heat that would—

Her breath caught as he entered her mouth. The exquisitely erotic sensation was even more than she'd anticipated.

They danced together. There was no awkward fumbling, no confusion on direction or pacing. Instead they moved with a rhythm that seemed as old as time.

She tilted her head to allow him to deepen the kiss. She wanted more. She wanted all of it. She wanted his hands on her body, hers on his and plenty of rubbing and plunging to go along with that touching. She never wanted the kiss to end.

Even as he urged her closer, she melted into him. Needing. Wanting.

He tasted of Scotch and their chocolate dessert. She wanted to know what the rest of him would taste like. She wanted to explore his body and have him—

Rational thought returned and with it a semblance

of emotional sanity. Regretful, she drew back a little. Eric got the message instantly and broke the kiss.

They stared at each other in the diffused light of the parking lot. Hannah was gratified to notice that his breathing was as rapid and uneven as her own. She would hate to think she'd been the only one blown away by their kiss.

Eric's eyes were dark, his mouth damp. She could see the quick rise and fall of his chest. He looked like a man with bed on his mind, and she had a feeling she looked just as hungry.

The proximity of her hotel room gave her pause for about seven seconds, but then reality pushed to the front of the line and reminded her that there were a dozen reasons not to take this any further.

For one thing, crush or no crush, she barely knew Eric, and sex with strangers had never been her style. For another, about four months ago, she'd thought she'd been madly in love with someone. That had proven to be a mistake, but she would do well to remember that her judgment in the male department wasn't always the best. Finally, dating while keeping her pregnancy a secret was one thing, but physical intimacy without coming clean would just be tacky.

"I didn't mean for that to get out of hand," Eric said quietly. "While I find you attractive, I wasn't prepared for the chemical reaction between us."

He'd felt it, too! She resisted the urge to cheer. "I know what you mean. We practically steamed the windows."

He smiled and touched her cheek. "I should have asked if I could see you again *before* we caught fire.

Now you're going to think I'm only in it for the kissing."

As if she would mind that kind of motivation. "I trust you to have substance," she said instead.

"Good. Then let's get together later this week. I'll give you a call."

"I'd like that."

He exited the car and came around to open her door. When she stepped out onto the parking lot, he closed the door behind her, then took her hand in his. Their fingers laced together.

Hannah liked the feel of him walking next to her. She liked a lot of things. But recent events had shown her that it made sense to take things slowly. She'd just moved back home, and there were a lot of things to consider.

But all that really great reasoning faded into the wind when Eric paused at the elevator and lightly kissed her cheek. Instantly her knees began to wobble, and her resolve to be sensible…well, it just plain vanished.

"I'll be in touch," he promised.

She nodded. "'Night."

She touched the button for the elevator and sighed. She was old enough to know better, but that didn't mean she did. No doubt she would be counting the minutes until the phone rang.

Hannah returned to her hotel room after a morning spent looking at furniture for her living room. There were a surprising number of choices. She wanted something that would wear well with a growing child in the house, while still being attractive and comfortable.

After flipping through more samples of fabric than should be legal, she'd ordered a sofa and two matching chairs, which would be held for her until she had a closing date on the house. End tables had proven more of a challenge and she was still torn between two different styles.

But all thoughts of decorating flew out of her head the second she put her card key in the lock. As soon as she pushed open the door, she stared intently at the phone to see if the message light was blinking. When she saw it was, she couldn't help grinning like a fool.

Over the past couple of days, she and Eric had played phone tag. He'd called while she'd been out, and she'd called while he'd been in meetings. The previous evening he'd tried to get her while she'd been on the phone with a girlfriend from college. She'd hung up at ten forty-five only to find he'd left her a message, but it had been too late to call him back.

She knew her reaction was silly and possibly immature, but the tingles of anticipation were so much fun that she refused to mind. So what if she was acting like an adolescent with a crush on a cute boy? Eric had been her fantasy for at least five years, so she'd certainly earned her reaction now. She would think of it as a reward for good behavior.

Besides, anyone who kissed as great as he did deserved to be obsessed about a little bit!

She picked up the phone and pushed the buttons

for messages, then plopped on the bed. Her heart flopped over in anticipation as the computerized female voice led her through menu options. She selected ''Play back new messages,'' and waited.

''Hey, Hannah, it's Eric. So tell the truth. Have you left town and decided not to let me know? I'm looking forward to seeing you again, assuming we can ever connect long enough to have a conversation and set up the details.''

He left her his office number and hung up.

Hannah hesitated as the computer offered her the option of saving or deleting the message. There was a part of her that wanted to keep it on file so she could listen to his voice whenever she got the urge.

''Okay—too juvenile for the situation,'' she murmured as she punched in the number to delete the message. Then she pressed nine for an outside line and dialed Eric's office.

His assistant picked up on the first ring.

''It's Hannah, again,'' she said. ''I'm returning his call.''

Jeanne laughed. ''He's going to be really crabby that he's missed you again. In this case he's been in a meeting for hours. I think he needs kidnapping. Want to volunteer?''

''I'm not sure my kidnapping skills are up to the task. Maybe I should just leave another message. Would you please let him know I'll be in all afternoon?''

''I'll tell him as soon as he makes his escape.''

Hannah thanked her and hung up. Then, in an effort to distract herself from waiting to hear from him, she collected the wallpaper sample books she'd picked up the previous afternoon and dropped them on the bed. She was sure she could lose herself in the joy of stripes and florals, with a couple of baby border prints thrown in for interest.

A couple of hours later, she knew she'd been lying. Sure, getting the house together was important, but right now her hormones had other things on their mind. Namely a tall, dark, handsome former friend who made her blood race and her knees give way. She had it bad.

Hannah flopped back on the bed and hugged a pillow to her chest. What was wrong with her? While she'd always liked guys and enjoyed dating, she'd never allowed them to interfere with her goals. But Eric had always been different. From the first time she'd met him down by the lake, she'd been entranced. She'd wanted—

The phone rang. Hannah sucked in a breath, then reached for it. After letting it ring one more time—so she wouldn't seem *too* eager—she picked up the receiver.

"Hello?"

"Hi, it's Eric. You're a difficult lady to track down. You must be off doing secret stuff."

She smiled. "I like the idea of being a woman of mystery, but alas, I've just been out buying furniture. What about you? Jeanne said you needed a good kidnapping."

"She wasn't far wrong. Did you offer to take care of it?"

Hannah chuckled. "I was concerned I wouldn't do

it right, and a kidnapping is not something you want to mess up.''

''Good point. Are you more comfortable with dinner? I should be able to get out of here by six-thirty.''

She rolled toward her nightstand. ''And what time did you start this morning?''

''Seven.''

She winced. ''Gee, nearly a twelve-hour day.''

''I know. It's a little less time than I usually put in but you're worth it.''

''Thanks.'' She wanted to ask him why he put in such long hours, but she already knew the answer. He hadn't gotten to his current position by doing *less* than everyone else.

''So what about dinner?''

''I would love to. But it's my turn to provide the meal. As I'm currently without a kitchen, I can't cook, but I can offer a lovely room-service menu.''

There was a long pause on the other end of the phone. Hannah sat up.

''Would it help if I reminded you I have a suite, complete with living room and dining table?'' she asked.

''It doesn't make the invitation less interesting, but it takes away any ambiguity.''

She glanced down at the bed. As attracted as she'd been to Eric, she wouldn't be inviting him back to her room if it hadn't been a suite. With only a bed he would be too much of a temptation—not to mention a complication. Better to play things safe.

''Was that a yes?'' she asked.

''It was. Say seven?''

''Great. I'm looking forward to this.''

"Me, too."

More than was sensible, but he didn't have to know that.

Eric arrived ten minutes early. He thought about sitting out in his car until seven, just to be cool, but he wanted to see Hannah too much. All day during his meetings he'd been unable to keep his mind a hundred percent on his work. Thoughts of her had flashed in and out of his consciousness like a light show.

He shifted the flowers he'd brought from his right hand to his left, then knocked on the hotel room door.

Seconds later it opened, then Hannah was standing in front of him, smiling.

She looked good. Better than good. Dark slacks skimmed over her slender hips and long legs. A loose green sweater the same color as her eyes fell to just below her waist. Color stained her cheeks and her mouth... Just the way it curved up at the corners made him want to lean close and kiss her. Hard.

He settled on a greeting followed by a gentle kiss on her cheek, then handed her the flowers.

"One of my traditional moments," he said.

"They're beautiful. I'll call down for a vase when we order dinner." She stepped back and let him into the room. "Come and see the beauty of the Lakeside Inn."

He glanced around at the good-size living room. There was a kitchenette at one end, complete with a tidy table for two.

"Very nice," he told her.

"It's not home, but it will get me through until I'm in the house." She lowered her voice and leaned toward him. ''Plus, the coolest thing happens here. While I'm gone during the day, fairies appear and tidy up everything. It's so amazing.''

He laughed. ''If only it could be like that in the real world.''

''Exactly. I probably shouldn't tell you this, but I was a real slob in college. I've gotten better, but I still tend to leave things lying around. Which makes the visiting fairies even more fun.'' She motioned to the sofa. ''Have a seat, then I'll tell you what the specials are tonight at Chez Hannah.''

Eric waited until she'd set down the flowers and perched on one edge of the sofa before he settled on the other. She handed him the open room-service menu, but instead of glancing at it, he looked at her.

''You don't have to buy me dinner,'' he said firmly.

''What if I want to?''

''Not necessary.''

Her full mouth curved at the corners. ''But if I cooked, you wouldn't object.''

He considered that. ''True.''

''Eric, have you thought this through? If I cooked at home, not only would I be buying the food and paying for it, but there would also be labor involved. So ordering room service is really a lot easier.''

He shifted on the sofa. ''Maybe, but...''

She held up a hand. ''I know. It's the signing for the check part. Can't I tell you to just avert your eyes?''

''I don't think so.''

''You're a pretty typical guy.''

''Like I said—traditional.''

"Are you trustworthy and honest, too?"

"I try to be."

She sighed. "Okay, then I concede on room service, but only on the condition that the second I close escrow at the house, I fix you dinner."

He liked that she was planning for them to see each other again. "Works for me."

"So now that dinner's on you, I guess you can order what you want." She waved at the menu. "What looks good?"

Given a choice between an entrée and Hannah, it wasn't much of a choice. However, she wasn't offering herself, and he didn't think he should make the suggestion, so he studied the pages in front of him.

Five minutes later they'd placed their order, including the request for a vase for the flowers. Hannah fixed him a Scotch from the minibar.

"I feel like I'm on an airplane," he teased. "Want to pass me over a bag of peanuts."

She sorted through the small basket of snacks on top of the minibar. "I can only find a box of animal crackers. I don't think they're the same."

"Not really."

She returned to her seat and stretched out with her feet on the coffee table. He did the same.

"So tell me about your day," she said, glancing at him. "You're sure in a lot of meetings."

"That's a big part of what I do. I work with different departments, coordinating projects. There are also staff meetings, planning meetings, budget meetings."

Hannah wrinkled her nose. "And I thought law

school was a lot of time spent sitting and listening to people talk. Do you enjoy what you do?''

He nodded. ''Now that I'm a director, I have more impact. If a department of mine is in trouble, either with staffing problems or budget concerns, I can make decisions that turn things around. At the hospital we can't only be worried about the bottom line. Our mandate is to provide quality health care. It complicates the issues, which increases the challenge and I—'' He broke off and smiled sheepishly. ''I just got carried away.''

Hannah angled toward him and tucked her legs close to her body. ''No, I like it. Your enthusiasm for what you do is a tangible presence in the room. I don't know that I was ever so enthralled with law school. Probably one of the reasons I left. So you don't mind your long hours?''

''No.'' Work was the best part of his day. ''I'm willing to work hard and that's made a real difference for me.''

''The reason you moved up the food chain so quickly?''

''Part of it. There were also a few good breaks, some great timing and luck.''

She shook her head. ''I think it was more about putting in the hours than luck. Is it difficult being so much younger than everyone at your level?''

Eric considered the question. When his sister tried to talk about his work, he mostly gave her easy answers, because he didn't want her worrying. For the first time in a long time, he was tempted to tell the truth.

Hannah leaned toward him and lightly touched his

arm. ''Is that too personal a question? We can talk about something else.''

''It's fine. I'm figuring out how to explain what happens at work. Sometimes I'm considered the cocky kid who needs to earn his way into the inner circle. Other times I'm seen as innovative with a lot of new and fresh ideas. So there are pluses and minuses to the situation.''

''Like so many things in life.''

''Yeah. I made the decision to get my MBA because I knew it would help me advance. Some people resent that.''

She frowned. ''Even though they could go get one if they wanted to?''

''Uh-huh.''

''That doesn't make sense.'' She sipped from her glass of water. ''Hey, wait a minute. When did you get your advanced degree? How could you have graduated from college, gotten your MBA *and* been promoted so quickly?''

''I got it in two years, while I was working.''

Her eyes widened. ''You couldn't have had much of a life.''

Which was putting it mildly. He'd worked forty- to fifty-hour weeks, attended classes at night, and studied on weekends.

''I wanted to get it done,'' he told her.

''What about sleep?''

''I figured I would catch up later.''

''Did you?''

''Do I look tired?''

She smiled. ''No. You look good, but you already knew that. So you busted your butt at college, then you got a great job and continued to excel. I think maybe there's a message there. Either you're extremely driven or you're out to prove something."

"Trying to psychoanalyze me?"

"Will it work?"

"You'll have to let me know."

Before she could respond, there was a knock on the door, followed by a call of "Housekeeping."

"The vase," Hannah said, scrambling to her feet.

Eric watched her cross to the door. He liked how she moved. Sometime while they'd been talking she'd kicked off her shoes. He stared at her bare feet, which were surprisingly sexy.

As she set the vase on the kitchen counter and slipped the spray of flowers into the glass, he considered her last question. Was he driven or out to prove something?

Did it matter? As long as he ended up a professional success, he would consider his life a win.

After dinner Hannah suggested they return to the sofa. The small table and chairs, while practical, didn't offer much room to spread out.

"I heard from the escrow company this afternoon," she said as she sat on the sofa. "With everything signed, they're saying we can close next week."

Eric nodded. "I had the same message. We can hold off a few days if you need more time to prepare."

"I appreciate that, but no thanks. I'm ready to get on with the next stage of my life."

"Planting those berries?"

She laughed. ‘‘You bet. I’ve already picked out how many plants I want and where they’re going.’’

‘‘Let me know if you need some help with the heavy labor.’’

His offer pleased her *and* surprised her. ‘‘You don’t strike me as the gardening type.’’

‘‘I’m a man of many talents.’’

She briefly thought of the kiss they’d shared and knew he was right. The thought of them hanging out together, digging in the soil, teasing and laughing, made her insides tighten with anticipation.

The sensible part of her brain told her not to take things too quickly with Eric. She’d made that mistake with Matt and look at what had happened. This time she wanted to be sure that she and the man she was interested in both believed that they should come first in each other’s lives.

‘‘Do you think you’ll get a boat?’’ he asked.

It took her a second to mentally segue back into the conversation. ‘‘I don’t know if I remember how to sail.’’

‘‘Hey, you had a terrific instructor. You should remember everything.’’

Hannah grinned as she recalled those afternoon lessons in the small boats available for rent. She’d been far more interested in her instructor than in the activity itself.

‘‘Hate to disappoint you,’’ she said. ‘‘But I suspect it’s one of those use-it-or-lose-it skills.’’

He shook his head. ‘‘Sailing is like riding a bike. You may be a little rusty, but you don’t forget. Let me know if you want to get a boat. We can rent one first, and you can practice.’’

More time spent together? Her heart gave a little *ping* of appreciation.

"A very nice invitation. I'll let you know if I get the urge to spend my days on the lake."

Actually, the activity sounded like fun. Of course, come midsummer, she would be showing and a lot more awkward. She supposed in that condition, having her on a sailboat would be a hazard.

"Your old summer job must have been a lot of fun," she said. "But I always wondered how you learned to sail in the first place."

She knew there was no way his mother had been able to afford lessons.

"I started out working in the snack shack," he said easily. "No skills required there. When I found out how much more sailing instructors made, I started hanging out with those guys. They would take me out on the lake after closing and show me the basics. I spent a lot of off hours practicing, and when I was good enough, I applied for a job."

"That took a lot of initiative."

"I was motivated," he admitted. "I had to pay for my car and save for college. That meant long hours on the lake."

She remembered those summer days. "Most of your students were pretty girls. I don't think you actually suffered all that much."

Humor made his eyes crinkle, even though he didn't smile. "I have no idea what you're talking about. I was putting in ten- and twelve-hour days."

"Right. Floating around with a bunch of bikini-clad teenage girls to keep you company. Talk about tough duty. And when you finally docked, you had your own private harem to follow you around wherever you went.''

''You're embarrassing me,'' he protested.

She took in the faint smirk and pleased expression. ''Oh, I don't think so. I suspect you're proud of your past. Harem and all.''

''I think you're exaggerating. Anyway, you managed not to be impressed,'' he reminded her.

''Not exactly.''

He stared at her in shock. ''What are you talking about? We were friends.''

She laughed. ''*You* were friends. I had a mad crush on you.'' She sighed. ''It was very sad. All those summers of unrequited love. It would have made a great movie.''

Eric looked as if he'd been blindsided. ''I never knew.''

''I didn't want you to. I figured out pretty quickly you weren't interested in me that way, so what was the point of saying anything? I would rather have been your friend. Besides, the other girls came and went with the regularity of the tide while I lasted for several years.''

''But you were so young.''

''Maybe when we first met, but I was eighteen that last summer.''

His expression changed from surprised to predatory. ''You should have said something.''

''You wouldn't have been interested back then.''

''What if I am now?''

Then there was every possibility all her dreams would come true. She tilted her head.

''Are you?''

He moved closer and slipped an arm around her. Instantly, every cell in her body sighed in total happiness.

"More than interested," he murmured as he drew her against him.

She supposed that more kissing was safe enough. She would stay strong and not give in to the powerful attraction she felt whenever Eric was within fifty feet of her person. She would resolve to act like an adult and not swoon like a giddy teenager.

Her good intentions lasted right up until he kissed her.

Chapter Five

Eric brushed her mouth with a combination of possession and tenderness that made her insides melt. Intense memories of their last kiss combined with the sensual sensations of the current one, swirling and combining until she couldn't tell past from present. All she could do was...*want.*

Need flooded her as her entire body focused on every point of contact. There was the pressure of his mouth against hers, the soft warmth of his breath on her cheek, the delicious grate of stubble. One of his hands settled on her shoulder while the other cupped her hip. Her legs nestled against his, her hands clung to his upper arms.

A general sort of "Take me now!" ache took up residence in her breasts. Between her legs she felt heat and pressure. All this in the first eighteen seconds, she thought, trying desperately to hold on to some kind of control. What would happen after a full minute?

There was no time to consider an answer to the question because just then she felt the gentle touch of his tongue on the seam of her mouth. She couldn't part for him fast enough.

The first exquisite brush of his tongue against hers made her shiver. She strained closer, wanting him to touch her everywhere. Now! She clung to him, fighting the need to moan and squirm. Eric made a noise low in his throat that let her know he was fighting the same kind of urges.

He wrapped his arms about her waist and drew her onto his lap. She leaned into him, letting her hip nestle against his belly, and lower, where she felt the hard stirrings of his desire.

One of his hands stroked her back, the other rested on her thigh. She touched his jaw, his neck, then ran her fingers through his hair.

"Hannah," he breathed against her mouth. "I can't believe what I was missing all those years ago."

She smiled and nipped at his lower lip. "I was shier then."

"So was I."

Somehow she doubted that, but she didn't say anything, not when he'd moved his hand to rest on her shoulder. His fingers lightly stroked the hollow of her throat. From there it was a very short walk to her breasts.

But Eric didn't go there. Instead he returned his attention to her mouth, where he kissed her with a thoroughness that left her shaken down to her bones.

She needed and wanted and found it difficult to breathe. Passion flooded her, intense and almost unfamiliar.

It had never been like this before, she thought hazily. Not with her few boyfriends in college and never with Matt. Matt who had told her he loved her and had nearly convinced her to marry him.

But she didn't want to think about Matt right now. Or her past, or anything but how feeling Eric's arousal pushing against her hip made her want to straddle him and welcome him home. She wasn't usually one for casual sex, but certainly exceptions could be made for these very specific circumstances.

Even as her body produced arguments as to why it was such a swell idea to rip off her clothes and give in, her brain reminded her that this was only their second date and that Eric, charming and appealing as he might be, was a relative stranger and that she was just about four months pregnant with another man's baby.

Reality splashed over her like ice water, making her aware of her surroundings. She still wanted to give in, but she knew she couldn't. Not this quickly.

But the wanting was still there, so she reached down and covered his hand with hers, then moved it so that he cupped her right breast.

Strong fingers closed over her sensitive curves. His thumb brushed against her nipple and she whimpered. Ribbons of sensation wove their way through her body before settling between her legs. She had a feeling it was probably illegal to want a man this much.

Regretfully, almost painfully, she drew back. Eric broke the kiss, and they stared at each other. His dark eyes seemed almost black. Fire flickered in the depths of his pupils. Tension drew his mouth into a straight line, and the hardness pressing against her hip flexed.

''Moving a little fast?'' he asked, the light tone of his voice a direct contrast to the tension in their bodies.

She nodded.

''I understand,'' he told her. ''It's only our second date. Of course all this is your fault.''

''What?'' She slid off of his lap and glared at him. ''Why is it my fault?''

He grinned and touched her cheek. ''Because you're so damned tempting. How am I supposed to resist?''

Oh. Blame like that she could handle. ''Yes, well, you have your own share of charm,'' she admitted. ''I think the blame is pretty evenly shared.''

His expression turned serious. ''I'm not trying to push you,'' he said quietly. ''This got a little out of hand tonight, which isn't what I had planned. I'll back off, and we'll take things more slowly.''

She was a swirling cauldron of emotions. On the one hand, *she'd* been the one settling his fingers on her breast, so that part really wasn't his fault. On the other hand, she loved that he respected her feelings and wanted to take things slowly. If she were some kind of alien creature with more than two hands, she would also add the fact that taking things more slowly meant seeing each other again. It was a plan she could really get behind.

''Slower works,'' she told him.

''Good.''

He rose and pulled her to her feet, then lightly

kissed her mouth. ''I'm going to get out of here before I give in to temptation and start ripping at clothes.''

''Better clothes than body parts,'' she said lightly.

Eric chuckled and led the way to the door.

''I'll call you tomorrow,'' he said.

''I'll look forward to it.''

He let himself out and Hannah locked the door behind him. Then she giggled as if she was still fourteen and raced to the sofa where she threw herself across the cushions.

''I think he likes me,'' she whispered into the silence. ''Isn't that totally cool?''

Good sense in the form of second thoughts returned at about 10:17 the next morning. Hannah sat at the small desk in the hotel suite living room and tried to get her life in order. Barring that, she would settle for organizing the move. Except she was having a heck of a time not thinking about Eric.

What was there about the man that made her heart beat faster? Was it his good looks? That he was basically a nice guy? The past? Or did all those factors combine to make her crazy?

She knew she couldn't rush headlong into this relationship. Not after her disaster the last time she'd followed her heart. Not that Matt and Eric were anything alike. Matt had been smooth and sophisticated, all East Coast charm. Eric was someone she'd known for years. She knew his history, his values. Sure, he'd had lots of girlfriends, but he'd never used any of them for anything. Matt had been out for what he could get.

Those last words opened the door to her wounded heart. Taking a deep breath to brace herself, Hannah gingerly poked at the healing sore and was surprised to find it much less painful than she would have thought.

Remembering Matt no longer made her want to cry, or scream. She could acknowledge her mistake and even see how it had happened. She knew now she'd been the perfect target for his brand of seduction. With the knowledge of hindsight she would be able to see through his facade, but six months ago she'd been a lot less wary.

Her speedy recovery made her both happy and sad. Sure it was great not to wake up in emotional agony every morning, but if she'd gotten over Matt this quickly, had she ever really loved him? And if she hadn't, what was she going to say to her child?

She patted her slightly rounded tummy and smiled. "I guess the two of us won't be having any serious heart-to-heart conversations anytime soon, huh? In the meantime, I can work on getting the wording right."

Until then, she had plenty to deal with. Not only her growing attraction to Eric and what that might mean, but also her family. She couldn't hide from them forever.

Hannah slumped down in the chair. Calling her grandmother and informing her she'd moved back to town permanently, *without* her law degree did not fill her heart with joy. In fact it made her a little queasy. And as she'd yet to have a speck of morning sickness, she knew the icky sensation in her stomach came from nerves, not hormones.

Not that Myrtle would yell or even speak loudly. In fact, she would probably *say* all the right things. But that didn't mean her disapproval wouldn't show in her eyes.

At times like this, Hannah really missed her mother. Eleven years after her death, Hannah still mourned all that they'd both lost. Not that her mom would have approved of the current direction of Hannah's life, but she would have tried to understand and be supportive. She would also have been able to offer wonderful advice about the realities of raising a child as a single mother.

Hannah thought of her own childhood. There might not have been a lot of money, but she'd never really noticed. Their tiny house had been happy and cheerful. If special days were marked by modest celebrations, she hadn't minded. There'd been enough love, and that's what she remembered now. The feeling of being the most important part of her mother's life.

"That's what I want for you," Hannah whispered. "I'll love you with my whole heart."

And do everything she could to make that enough. She'd grown up without a father and turned out okay. So had Eric. She frowned. Had he minded not having a man around the house?

The obvious way to get her question answered was to ask him directly, but she wasn't sure she was ready for that. Their budding relationship still lacked definition. Eric seemed to enjoy her company and, judging from his sensual kisses and obvious arousal, he liked her body as well. But for how long? What would change when she told him she was pregnant and had no plans to ever see the father of her baby again?

She had a feeling the truth was going to turn things around big-time. Would Eric still want to be physically intimate if he knew about the baby? Didn't a lot of men think pregnant women were unattractive? Would he judge her for allowing all this to happen and think she was a flake for getting over Matt so quickly?

Hannah rested her elbows on the desk. She had to let this go. She was wasting too much time thinking and not enough doing. So she would make her lists then start to get things done. As for Eric and what *he* might think, she could speculate all she wanted but until they had a conversation about it, she would never know. The mature choice would be to tell him the next time she saw him.

Sensible, too, she told herself, but something inside of her recoiled at the thought. There was no excuse—she was just plain scared. Scared of being judged and found wanting. Scared of being compared to her father, who got her mother pregnant and then walked away from them both.

In Eric's mind, the old neighborhood where he'd grown up hadn't changed much in the past ten years. The houses had gotten a little older, as had most of the residents. The streets were still narrow, the trees tall and nearly touching over the parked cars, the yards and the painfully neat walkways.

It was a section of town that catered to those on hourly salaries—the proud and determined residents who could never put enough money away to take them through every emergency.

He pulled into the narrow driveway to the side of the recently painted house. Until he'd gone away to college, he'd never lived anywhere but here. Nearly all of his childhood memories were tied up in the structure, yet he'd been surprised at how easily somewhere else had become home.

Now he stepped out onto the driveway, carrying a bottle of wine and a small toolbox. As he had every Sunday since his sister had moved back three years before, he'd shown up to eat dinner with her and make any minor repairs to the old place.

Eric walked up the front steps. The railing was new—he'd replaced it the previous fall. There were planter boxes, which made him think of Hannah and her obsession with growing berries. His sister Cecilia—CeCe—liked to garden as well, but her hectic schedule didn't leave her a whole lot of free time. Not that he was one to point fingers in the long-hours department.

He knocked, then opened the front door and stepped inside.

"Hey, sis, it's me," he called.

"In the kitchen," CeCe yelled back. "Wipe your feet."

He grinned as he carefully used the mat right in front of the door. Older by eleven years, CeCe had always been as much parent as sister. When their mother had gotten sick and CeCe had moved home, his sister had taken the role to new heights. But Eric didn't complain. Not when CeCe had shouldered the burden of tending their mother during her lingering illness so he could finish his education and start his life. He owed her. So when their mother had died, he'd signed his half of the old house over to her.

"Tell me you're grilling steaks," he said as he walked into the bright, cheery kitchen.

CeCe, a pretty, dark-eyed brunette who barely came to his shoulder, smiled at him. "That is never going to happen, Eric. Red meat will kill you."

"You don't know that for sure. I think we should test the theory with a nice, juicy steak. I'll even crank up the barbecue, if you're afraid of fire."

She shook her head and reached for him. "You're such a pain. Why do I love you?"

"You can't resist."

He stood still while she cupped his face and studied his features. "You look tired," she announced. "And you're not eating right. When was the last time you had a vegetable?"

"There was a tomato on the hamburger I ate yesterday. Oh, and lettuce."

She sniffed. "Lettuce isn't a vegetable."

"Sure it is. It's green. Anything green is a vegetable. Jeanne keeps jelly beans on her desk and I make sure to eat plenty of the green ones, just so you won't have to worry."

She released him. "Eric, you're not a kid anymore. You need to take care of yourself better."

"Quit fussing."

He set the wine on the counter, and the toolbox on the floor. Then he grabbed his sister in a bear hug and squeezed until she huffed in protest. When he let her go, she slapped at his hand, but he read the love in her eyes.

"So what's the plan?" he asked. "Where's the leak? In the tub or the sink?"

"The sink. I'm sure it's a washer. I'm about to put on the pasta, so you can fix it after dinner."

"Yes, ma'am."

She narrowed her gaze. "Are you sassing me?"

"Probably."

He headed for the sink and washed his hands. While she stirred the pasta into boiling water, he walked to the cupboards and began removing dishes.

After their mother had died, CeCe had decided to keep the house. Over the past couple of years, she'd made some changes—painting the walls, replacing the secondhand sofa with something new and bright. She also liked to restore antiques, and he saw she'd finished the sideboard he'd helped her with over the winter.

But some things stayed the same, he thought as he collected dishes from the cupboard they'd been in since he could remember.

"Looks good," he said, tilting his head toward the sideboard.

CeCe smiled. "I'm happy with how it came out. There's a bedroom set I've been eyeing at the secondhand store. It's from the forties and would look great." She shrugged. "I'm still thinking."

Eric put the dishes on the oak table and crossed to stand next to her. "If it's about the money," he began.

She cut him off with a shake of her head. "It's about time. I'm not sure I want to commit to refinishing that much furniture right now."

"I could help."

"I don't think so, but I appreciate the offer."

"So I'm good enough for the basics like fixing a leak, but I'm not good enough for fancy work, like refinishing furniture?"

His sister considered the question, then nodded. "That's exactly right."

He chuckled. "Gee, thanks."

She pointed at the dishes. "The table isn't going to set itself, young man."

"You're bossy."

"It's a point of pride where you're concerned."

He finished the table while she continued to stir the pasta. After opening the wine and pouring it into their glasses, Eric carried the salad and bread to the table.

When she announced it was time, he drained the pasta and poured it onto a serving plate. CeCe spooned on a creamy tomato and salmon sauce.

Once they were seated, Eric started silently counting in his head. Right on schedule, somewhere between six and seven seconds after their fannies were planted in the chairs, CeCe launched her attack.

"I don't understand why you have to work so many hours," she said as she passed him the pasta. "I see the light on in your office when I get to the clinic, and it's always still on when I leave."

He loved his sister more than he'd ever loved anyone, but she made him crazy. "Sis, I come over here for dinner nearly every week and as soon as we start to eat, you tear into me. Couldn't we talk about something simple and easily resolved, like the conflicts in the Middle East?"

Her gaze narrowed. "Very funny. I worry about you."

"I worry about you, too. You've been alone too long. It's twisting your brain."

"This conversation isn't about me. It's about you and the impossible hours you work. It was one thing when you were working on your MBA while holding down a full-time job. Then you didn't have a choice. But now you do. You need balance in your life, Eric. You need to *get* a life."

"You don't have much beyond your work," he said, hoping to distract her.

"I have hobbies and friends, and at least I was married before. You're getting to that age when it's important to start thinking about your long-term goals."

"I have plenty of those."

Her mouth twisted. "I'm not talking about career goals. I mean personally. Don't you want to get married? Don't you want to have children?"

He chewed on a piece of salmon and considered her question. Kids? Sure. He'd always wanted kids. But he was less sure about the whole wife thing. From his perspective, love didn't last and then people went away. It's not as if CeCe's marriage had been anything but a disaster. Except for his secretary, he didn't know anyone who was happily married.

Unfortunately, that argument wouldn't work with CeCe. Sometimes, when she got on a roll, it was easier to step out of the way. He was about to concede defeat and tell her she was right when he remembered he had some ammunition of his own.

"I'm seeing someone," he told her.

CeCe paused in the act of sipping her wine and stared at him over her glass. "Are we talking dating here, or are you trying to pass off getting a new assistant?''

''Real dates,'' he said holding up both hands in a gesture of victory. ''With kissing and everything.''

CeCe looked suspicious. ''What's wrong with her?''

He winced. ''Because only someone with problems would want to date your only brother? That's cold.''

''No. That's not what I meant. You never date women who are interested in anything but having a good time. I assume she's like that?''

Eric hadn't determined where Hannah stood on the ''good times only'' scale. If they were going to keep seeing each other, they were going to have to have that conversation. And he had plans to keep seeing her. It had been a long time since a woman had gotten his attention in such a huge way. In fact, he couldn't remember it happening ever before.

''She's great,'' he said, sidestepping the question. ''Beautiful, smart, funny. I knew her back when I worked at the lake.''

''Do I know her? What's her name?''

''Hannah Bingham.''

CeCe wrinkled her nose. ''One of them, huh? Be careful, Eric. There's something about that family.''

''No, she's not like that. Hannah wasn't born rich. She's one of Billy Bingham's kids. She didn't know he was her dad until she was about thirteen or fourteen. She's okay. Better than okay.''

CeCe's expression turned speculative. ''Sounds like you have it bad.''

He did, but not in the way his sister meant, and

there was no way he was going to discuss his sexual interest in Hannah with CeCe.

"So you're dating?" she asked.

"Yes."

"Seriously?"

"It's been a couple of weeks. Give me a break."

"All right. I'll back off. But it wouldn't kill you to fall in love."

He ignored that. "All right. Enough with the torture. Tell me what's going on in your life. How's work?"

"Busy. People keep having babies."

CeCe had been a practicing midwife for years. She loved her work and had been the one to teach Eric how important it was to have a passion for what he did with his day.

"Things going okay?" he asked.

CeCe nodded, then sighed. "They are for me, but the clinic..."

"What?"

Her eyes darkened with sadness. "There were some problems with a home birth a few months ago. Now the parents are making trouble."

Eric understood the significance of her statement. The area home birthing program was unique. Healthy, risk-free expectant mothers could choose to have a home birth, if they preferred. Specially trained midwives were on hand to aid and assist.

"What happened?" he asked. "Were you..."

She cut him off with a half smile. "I'm okay. I wasn't involved. It was Milla. She's amazing and very thorough. Apparently the birth was completely normal, but the parents didn't pay attention when she told them how to clean the umbilicus, and they never brought their child in for any postnatal care. The baby ended up sick and in intensive care. Now they're suing the clinic and Milla. They say she didn't cut the cord properly or instruct them on how to care for it."

While the clinic and the hospital were technically separate facilities, they were not only physically connected by a glassed-in walkway, they were also symbiotically connected through practices, patients and personnel. Eric knew that a lawsuit over something like this could devastate both the clinic and Milla.

"How's Milla doing?" he asked.

"Not great. Something like this could end her career." CeCe shook her head. "I understand that our profession is such that a mistake can have tragic consequences. Which is why we're so careful all the time. But to prosecute Milla when she did everything right makes no sense."

"Sometimes people can't accept responsibility for what they've done. They find it easier to blame others."

"That's wrong."

"I agree." He touched her arm. "Anything I can do to help?"

"I don't know. Maybe. Talking helps. You getting married would help."

He stared at her. "How would my marriage change the situation in any way?"

"It would give me a distraction." She chuckled. "Face it, Eric. You owe me, big-time. So as a favor to your only sister, I think you should get married."

"You first."

"Like that's going to happen."

"You never know."

He would like to see his sister happy and settled with someone. As for himself, while he wasn't interested in forever, he was very intrigued by Hannah. He might not want to get her down the aisle, but finding her in his bed would be a definite bright spot.

Chapter Six

Tuesday morning Hannah arrived at Eric's office to pick up the keys to her new home. Escrow had closed late the previous afternoon, and she was now the proud owner of her very first house.

She'd thought she might be nervous about taking such a big step, but instead she found herself excited and sure of her decision. Now if only she could decide on the window coverings for the downstairs bedrooms.

"You look cheerful," Jeanne said as Hannah walked into the foyer. "How much of that is about taking possession today and how much of it is about a certain handsome guy we both know?"

Hannah laughed. "Can I get back to you on the exact percentages?"

"Sure thing." Jeanne rose and pointed to the row

of chairs by the wall. "Have a seat. He's on a conference call that's scheduled to go for a couple more minutes. He asked me to ask you if you would please wait." Jeanne winked. "I'm not making that up, either. He used the *P* word and everything."

Hannah settled on one of the padded chairs. "Eric is very polite."

"Uh-huh. You want some coffee?"

"No, thanks."

Jeanne took the seat across from her and leaned forward. "Polite is the least of it," she said, her voice low. "Can we agree on good-looking and a great catch?"

Hannah tried not to smile. "Don't you think he's capable of getting his own girls?"

"Sure, but does he?" Her expression turned rueful. "Not that one. He would rather be working late than out with an attractive woman. Or at least that was his preference until recently. Hmm, I wonder what's changed? Could it be you?"

"I'm not sure I'm willing to take the responsibility for that. Eric's lots of fun, and we enjoy our time together. But it's only been a couple of dates."

A couple of dates that ended in very steamy kisses, she thought as her mind flashed on what had happened after their dinner in her hotel room. Just thinking about it practically gave her a hot flash.

"You might want to consider more dates," Jeanne said. "I rag on Eric all the time but the truth is, he's a great guy. And he needs someone to love him."

Hannah didn't want to touch that comment. From what she could see, Eric was more than self-sufficient.

Did he need someone to love him and would he be willing to love back?

"I'll think about it," Hannah said, not wanting to commit to more.

"Good." Jeanne grinned conspiratorially. "So, what's the inside of the Bingham mansion really like? Do they have hot-and-cold-running servants?"

Hannah laughed, then talked a little about the family home. "I never feel like I really belong there," she admitted. "I guess that's because I wasn't born to that kind of wealth."

"I guess that *could* be a problem," Jeanne said cheerfully. "But I would be willing to work darned hard to overcome it. Think Myrtle wants to adopt a middle-aged assistant as a sort of honorary sister?"

"I could ask."

"That would be great."

"What would be great?" Eric asked as he stepped out of his office. "Jeanne, are you torturing Hannah?"

"Just a little," his assistant said as she rose. "I think of it more as entertaining her."

Hannah stood and faced the man who had been haunting her dreams. She studied his face, searching for a flaw. There wasn't one. So if she couldn't fault his looks or his behavior then was it fair for anyone to hold her responsible for the fact that her crush on him was alive and well?

"Jeanne's terrific," Hannah said.

Eric pressed a finger to his lips. "Don't say that in front of her. She's already convinced I couldn't make it through my day without her."

''Could you?'' Hannah asked as he led her into his office.

''Probably not, but it's better if she doesn't know.'' He smiled at Jeanne. ''Please hold my calls.''

His assistant winked. ''Sure thing, boss.''

Eric closed the door.

Hannah faced him. ''I heard escrow closed yesterday.''

''It did. Congratulations. I have the keys right here, along with the final papers.''

He walked to his desk and picked up a large envelope. When she took it, she smiled.

''So it's official,'' she said happily.

''You're a home owner.'' He bent close and lightly kissed her mouth.

Hannah knew he meant the contact to be little more than a polite greeting, but that didn't stop her from feeling it right down to the tips of her toes.

''I am so in over my head with you,'' she said before she could stop herself.

Eric raised his eyebrows. ''Those are words every man likes to hear.''

''Really?''

''It beats 'let's just be friends.' Or was that coming next?''

She clutched the papers in front of her like a shield, then took a seat on the sofa. He sat next to her. All the while, she tried to figure out what she wanted to say.

''I know I should be mature and sophisticated,'' she told him. ''But I'm not.''

''We agreed to take things slowly,'' he reminded

her. "Is that the problem? Would you rather not see me again?"

"No!" She pressed her lips together. "No, it's not that. I just... It's confusing. I want things to go slowly. I think that's important. But at the same time, I can't help wishing they *weren't* going slowly. Does that make sense?"

"Not really. I can't decide if I should move to a chair across the room or attack you right here on the sofa."

Her first vote was for the attacking. But there were complications: the baby; Jeanne being in the next room; this was where Eric worked; anyone could walk in on them.

He tugged the envelope from her death grip and set it on the coffee table. Then he took one of her hands in his.

"Here's the thing," he said, staring into her eyes and making her want to melt. "I'm enjoying my time with you. While I find you attractive and I look forward to being physically intimate with you, I'm not only in this for sex."

She swallowed. He'd said sex. Just like that. "Good to know," she said, her voice a squeak.

He grinned. "Would you rather I said I *didn't* want you?"

Good point. "No."

"So we'll continue to see each other. As for the rest of it, the physical side of things, we'll back off on that. No heavy make-out sessions for a while. Sound good to you?"

He was being so great, she thought, more than a little dazed by the realization. Matt had only been out for what he could get, while Eric seemed genuinely interested in what *she* wanted. It was a startling concept.

"Works for me," she said. "You're being terrific."

"Hey, I'm a terrific guy. So when does the moving van arrive?"

"Thursday. I'm having the furniture delivered that day, too."

"What time should I be there?"

She blinked at him. "Eric, I said Thursday. That's a workday. You can't take the time off."

"Sure I can. Have you told your family you're back?"

"What? No. Just Ron and Mari know."

"I figured as much. So you don't have anyone to help. The movers will bring everything in, but what if you want to move furniture around after they're gone? I can take care of that. I'll be there around nine."

"That would be great. Really."

"My pleasure."

She didn't know what to think. Eric was a man who loved his career more than anything, yet he was willing to help her on a weekday. She didn't want to read too much into the offer, but she couldn't help thinking that coming home had been the right thing to do for more reasons than she'd realized.

Hannah was too excited to sleep Wednesday night, and she arrived at her new house early Thursday morning. After starting coffee for Eric and the moving guys in the coffeemaker she'd bought the previous day, she heated water for her tea, then walked around the empty rooms and imagined what they would look like filled with furniture.

It was a warm spring day. Bright, sunny and loud with the sounds of birds in the nearby trees. She'd opened most of the windows, and a soft breeze blew through the house. Her new berry plants were in place. She'd planted them after leaving Eric's office with the key. Flowers bloomed, and suddenly her life seemed filled with promise.

"We're going to be okay," she said, touching her stomach and imagining her baby. "Better than okay. We're going to have a good life in this house. I can feel it. But first, I have a lot of hard work ahead of me. Getting this house in order, for one."

Speaking of which…she glanced at her watch. The truck should be here shortly.

Just then she heard an engine, but she knew it was from a car, not a moving van. Even so, she moved to the front door and stepped outside. Sure enough, a sleek sedan pulled in next to her battered car, and Eric stepped out.

She'd had a long talk with herself the previous evening. She'd listed all the reasons why she shouldn't get involved with anyone right now. Even if he was tall, handsome, gentle and sexy enough to front a cult. But resolutions made while alone in her hotel room were one thing. Resolutions in the light of day and within sight of Eric's smile were something else.

"I brought doughnuts," he said as he stepped out of the car. "I didn't know which you liked so I got some of everything."

She laughed. "I'm pretty comfortable with anything wearing a doughnut label. But you're here to provide physical labor. You didn't have to bring food, too."

He walked toward her and opened the pink bakery box, then waved it under her nose. "Want me to take them back?"

"No. I don't think I could stand it."

She reached for a maple bar and he took a chocolate-covered glazed.

"I have coffee brewing," she said. "It should be ready."

"Lead me to it, and I'll be your slave forever. Or at least for the rest of the day."

"Right through here."

She led the way into the house. Once they were in the empty kitchen, Eric set down the box and poured himself a mug of coffee. It was only then that Hannah noticed what he was wearing.

Not the well-fitting suits she was used to. Nope, there wasn't a tie in sight. Instead Eric wore faded jeans that hugged his hips and emphasized the muscles in his thighs, along with a battered T-shirt that stretched across his broad shoulders.

Her heart did a little swan dive right there in her chest, and her palms began to sweat. She wanted to blame her reaction on hormones, and she was right. Unfortunately, this particular brand of internal chemicals had nothing to do with her pregnancy and everything to do with her wanting the man standing in front of her.

The good news was the low rumble of a truck climbing the hill distracted her, so she was able to take a step back and not embarrass herself by ripping off her clothes and begging him to take her right there, next to the doughnut box!

Unloading didn't take much time. Hannah hadn't bothered shipping a lot of the furniture she'd accumulated while in college and law school. Most of her pieces had been thirdhand at best. But there was the round oak kitchen table with the tile inset she'd found at an estate sale, her kitchen stuff, and a big old-fashioned desk that had been her father's. There were also dozens and dozens of boxes.

"What's in these?" Eric asked as he carried two into the living room. "Bricks?"

"Books. I'm something of a pack rat where books are concerned."

She pointed him to the growing stack in the corner.

Shortly after the movers finished, the furniture folks arrived. When her living room set was in place, the men set up her new bed and pushed the dresser against the wall. The new washer and dryer were installed and pronounced working. At quarter to twelve, she signed the last delivery receipt and closed the front door.

Eric stood in the middle of the living room. "Not bad for a morning's work," he said.

"I still need a lot of little things," she said as she walked toward him. "Lamps, rugs, a few occasional tables." Baby furniture, but she wasn't ready to discuss that.

Eventually she knew she had to, but not just yet. Not when letting him in on her little secret would change everything between them. She still had no idea how he was going to react. While he might not be that concerned, she doubted he would be thrilled beyond words. As she liked things exactly as they were, later was looking better than sooner in the telling department.

He leaned against the doorframe and folded his arms over his chest. ‘‘What exactly *is* an occasional table? Does the name mean you can’t use it every day? And if you do, does it send a letter of protest to someone of authority?’’

‘‘I believe so. I’ve heard the penalties can be really daunting. So I’ll make sure it only has part-time work in my house.’’

‘‘Good thinking.’’

He glanced around at the furniture, the boxes of books and the newly delivered television.

‘‘You didn’t bring down very many things,’’ he said. ‘‘I would have thought you’d have more.’’

She shook her head. ‘‘You’re forgetting I was at a girls’ boarding school until college, then in dorm rooms. Neither place was conducive to accumulating a lot of stuff. My last couple of years of college, I had an apartment, but nearly everything in it was very used and not worth moving. At the time I was more interested in cheap than anything else.’’

‘‘But you’re a Bingham. You have plenty of money.’’

Hannah stiffened slightly. She didn’t want this to be a sensitive subject but, after what had happened with Matt, she couldn’t help being wary. Telling herself Eric was nothing like him didn’t seem to make a difference.

‘‘There’s some money,’’ she admitted. ‘‘But not as much as everyone thinks. My father left me a trust fund. If I’m careful, I can live on it. And yes, it did pay for the house. But it's not a fortune. I certainly couldn't buy a penthouse apartment and enjoy the high life."

She watched him as she spoke, searching for some kind of reaction. Eric didn't seem overly shocked by her statements, or disappointed.

"You don't strike me as a high-life kind of woman," he told her. "If you were, you wouldn't have come back here."

"Good point."

"Want to get to work on the kitchen?"

She smiled. "Absolutely."

She followed him into the cheery room and tried not to yip with happiness. Okay, so Eric had passed the test. He wasn't in it for the money. That was good. Not that she'd worried, but Matt had shown her a whole different side of life…one she hadn't liked.

Yes, she knew she was lucky. The money from her father meant she got to make choices. She could stay home with the baby for several years and not worry about supporting herself. She appreciated that. But having financial security didn't seem to make what she was supposed to do with herself any clearer. While she planned to devote herself to her child, she couldn't help thinking she would be a much better mother if she had interests other than child raising.

"All right, my semi-independently wealthy young woman," Eric said as he opened a box of dishes and began unwrapping plates. "Now that you're here, in your new home, what do you want to do with yourself?"

"Just what I was thinking. Can you read my mind?"

"Not even close. It was the next logical question. I know you love your berries and all, but how much time will they take?"

"You'd better get off of me about my berries, mister. Especially if you expect me to share."

"Fair enough. But that doesn't answer the question. What are your plans?"

"I don't know," she admitted, taking the plates from him and loading the dishwasher. "Do I need a plan?"

"It helps."

She glanced at him. "Let me guess. You have multiple plans. Short-term, long-term and maybe something in between."

He laughed. "Of course. They're part of the reason I've been successful in my career. I want to get ahead as quickly as possible."

Hardly a surprise. "Are you really shooting for being a CEO one day?"

"Sure. Why not?"

"You want to run some big company?"

"I'd enjoy the challenge. In the meantime, I'm building my résumé."

"What about a personal life?" she asked.

"Now you sound like my sister. CeCe is always bugging me to settle down."

Hannah's stomach clenched. "And you don't want to?"

"I want to be a part of something," he admitted.

He finished emptying the box. After pulling open the bottom, he flattened it and set it on top of the kitchen table. Then he started on the next box.

''You're already a part of something,'' he said. ''So that need is met for you.''

''If you're talking about my family, I don't actually consider myself to be a member of the inner circle. I'm more of an accidental relative.''

''That's not true.''

She straightened and shrugged. ''Are you sure? My grandmother has always been sweet to me, but the truth is, I exist because her son screwed up. She's not going to be happy that I left law school.'' Or about the baby. ''I don't want to see the disappointment in her eyes, so I haven't even told her I'm back in town. Which means she could hear it from someone else, which will be disappointing in its own right. So here I am, afraid of my grandmother, without a plan or direction.''

He stepped toward her and touched her chin. ''You're doing great,'' he said quietly. ''You're in transition. That will change.''

She wanted to ask if he really believed that or if he was just being kind. As she was afraid of the answer, she kept the question to herself.

''If it doesn't, I'll come to you for planning lessons,'' she said.

He released her chin and returned to the unpacking. ''I can offer a few tips.''

She thought about how far he'd come in such a short period of time. ''Your sister must be very proud of you. Of all you've accomplished.''

''She is.''

''You're close?''

''Yeah.'' He smiled. ''We try to get together for dinner every week or so. She tells me everything that's wrong in my life and I fix stuff around the house. It works.''

''That's nice. Growing up, I always wanted a brother or sister. Someone to play with, that sort of thing.''

''CeCe is nearly eleven years older than me. She wasn't exactly a playmate.''

''I guess not, but she was there for you.''

''Sure.''

That's what she wanted, she thought. Family she could count on. Friends to care about. Maybe it wasn't a high-powered career, but it would be a start at a life she could be proud of.

She already had a family, but they weren't exactly close. It occurred to her that she shared some of the blame for that. Especially since she'd come back. She'd been avoiding everyone. Maybe it was time to change that.

On Monday Hannah made good on her vow and drove over to see her grandmother. Myrtle lived in the large house her husband had built in the early fifties. Various parts of the building had been updated over the years, but the graciousness of the mansion was visible in the sweeping front porch and elegant lines.

Hannah parked in front. As she climbed out of her car, she brushed off her wool skirt and tugged at her short jacket. She felt more than nervous…she felt unworthy. As if she should present herself at the back door. Like a delivery person or a servant.

Reminding herself that she was here to connect with her family didn't seem to help. Maybe it was how she was raised—on the poor side of town in a household that never quite made ends meet. Maybe it was being her father's bastard daughter.

Determined to be a Bingham at heart, she walked up to the front door and knocked. A uniformed maid let her in and ushered her into Myrtle's private sitting room.

Hannah had been in this large room before. Regardless of the season, a fire crackled cheerfully in the fireplace and there were always vases of fresh flowers on the various inlaid tables. Soft pinks and reds made the space seem cozy. An Oriental rug stretched across the hardwood floors.

Two small sofas and a wing chair made up a conversational area. Hannah knew that the chair was for her grandmother. She'd made the mistake of sitting in it once and had been gently but firmly told she was to take her place on one of the sofas.

The lesson had occurred during her first visit to the house. She'd been all of fourteen, still mourning the death of her mother and confused about Billy Bingham being her father. Myrtle had explained things to her, including the fact that it was thought that the best thing for her was to attend a private girls' school back East.

With the wisdom of hindsight, Hannah knew she'd received an exemplary education. At the time, she'd assumed she was being sent away.

The small door in the corner opened and her grandmother entered into the room. Myrtle Northrup Bingham might be within a year or two of eighty, but she still walked with the confidence of youth. Not one to try to hold back time with a surgeon's knife, she looked close to her age, but in the graceful way of a woman who had always been a beauty.

Seeing Hannah, she smiled and held out both hands. ‘‘No one told me you were in town, Hannah. This is a lovely surprise.’’

‘‘Thank you.’’ Hannah lightly squeezed her hands and kissed her cheek, then waited until her grandmother was seated before perching on the edge of the sofa. ‘‘I’ve been back for a few days now.’’ Or weeks.

Only a couple, she told herself, then did the math. Okay, nearly three.

‘‘Are you on holiday from law school?’’

‘‘I—’’ she swallowed ‘‘—no. I’ve left Yale. Permanently.’’

Myrtle’s only reaction was a slight raising of her eyebrows as she turned to the tea service left beside her chair. She poured two cups and passed one to Hannah.

‘‘I see.’’

‘‘Yes, well, I felt the need to settle. So I’ve bought a house. It’s lovely. I hope you’ll be able to come see it.’’

Myrtle offered a plate of tiny sandwiches.

‘‘No, thank you,’’ Hannah murmured. ‘‘My house isn’t that far from here. On the other side of town, but nothing around here is that great a distance. There are lovely views, and I have a garden. I’ve been working in it.’’ She suddenly noticed her ragged nails, the result of trimming hedges and hauling away the cuttings. She tucked her free hand under her jacket.

Her grandmother sipped her tea. When she put the

delicate cup back on the saucer, she sighed. "I thought you wanted to be a lawyer."

"I did. I still might, I'm not sure. There are some things I have to figure out."

The baby, for one. But she decided telling her grandmother about moving back to town and buying a house was enough of a shock. She would save the whole great-grandchild explanation for next time.

"Is there a young man? Did you move home to get married?"

"No. Not really."

As for there being someone, Hannah wasn't sure Eric counted. They were dating, but things were still fairly new. She wasn't ready to torture him by introducing him to the Binghams.

"I've never thought of you as idle, Hannah," her grandmother said. "You're a sensible girl. I'm sure you'll sort this all out. Since you've returned, have you had a chance to drive by the large park on the east side of town? There have been many improvements. One of my committees raised money to replace all the play equipment for the children."

Myrtle chatted on about the changes and her charity work. With each passing second, Hannah felt herself shrinking in her seat. Her grandmother's disappointment was practically a living creature in the room. The message was clear—you were given opportunities and you blew it.

Hannah didn't disagree. She'd screwed up big-time. Aware of that, she was trying to set her life to rights. Not that Myrtle was likely to care.

After forty-five minutes, Hannah excused herself, promised to visit again soon and practically ran for her car. So much for connecting with family. She would never belong with them. She was completely on her own.

"Except for you," she said, touching her stomach. "We'll be a family."

And Eric? Did he want to be a part of her world? Was he interested in loving and being loved? Because that's what she wanted more than nearly anything. A man to love her with his whole heart. She wanted to be first in someone's life.

Chapter Seven

Hannah felt lower than slime as she drove down the long driveway after leaving Myrtle, although she couldn't say for sure *what* exactly could be lower than slime. But whatever it was, she was that. And ungrateful, because it was true. She'd been given amazing opportunities and not used them to the fullest.

Except...except she wasn't sure she'd ever wanted to go to law school. She'd been pointed in that direction by Myrtle, guided by the softly spoken words, "This is what your father wanted."

How was she supposed to resist that? And she hadn't, until she'd grown so unhappy she'd had no choice but to get away.

She stopped at the driveway's intersection with the street to check for traffic. There was one car coming, and she waited until it passed.

But instead of driving by, the car pulled up next to hers. She instantly recognized the big, dark Mercedes and the man driving it.

The slightly tinted window slid down soundlessly, and Ron Bingham smiled at her. "I see you decided to come clean with your grandmother. How did it go?"

"I'm trying to figure out what's lower than slime, because that defines my current condition."

Her uncle winced. "Not good. Which makes you a young woman in need of rescuing, and I know just how to do it. Follow me."

He rolled up the window and backed onto the street before she could protest that she couldn't be good company right now. The best course of action would be for her to return to her house where she could curl up on the sofa with a box of tissues and a sad movie.

But Ron had already started down the road, so she checked for traffic, then followed him toward town. Ten minutes later he parked on the street by May's Dairy Hut and waited while she got out of her car.

Although Hannah had spent plenty of summer afternoons hanging out at May's during high school, she hadn't been back in years. Little seemed to have changed. There were still several picnic benches out front, a walk-up window and only space for two cars in the parking lot. As it was spring and a school day, there weren't any other customers.

Hannah walked toward her uncle. "Not that I don't appreciate the gesture," she said. "I really do. But I think I'm a little old for ice cream to fix my problems."

"That's because you haven't tried it," he said, taking her arm and leading her to the window. ''It cures a lot of ills. More people should respect the healing powers of a good hot-fudge sundae.''

Despite her worse-than-slime feelings, Hannah couldn't help laughing. ''I'll give it a try.''

''Smart move. Even if your problems are just as big when you're done, you've had ice cream. That can't be all bad, right?''

''Interesting point.''

She stepped up to the window and ordered a two-scoop hot-fudge sundae. Ron got a banana split. Treats in hand, they walked to the picnic benches and settled on one in the shade.

Hannah dug in. The first bite of cold ice cream and warm fudge nearly made her swoon. By bite three, things really didn't look so terrible. Maybe Ron was on to something.

Her uncle waited until she'd finished her first scoop and was well into her second before speaking.

''Want to talk about what happened with your grandmother?'' he asked.

She wiped her mouth with a napkin. ''Sure. There's not much to tell. Myrtle was lovely and gracious as always. Maybe this is all about me. My inner guilt projecting itself onto her. I don't know. It's just...'' She glanced at Ron. ''I'm not sure I ever wanted to be a lawyer.''

''That would make law school more difficult.''

''I'm not saying I don't,'' she added. ''I know. None of this makes sense. I guess the point is I don't know what I want. No one has ever asked me, and I've sure never asked myself. Okay, when I was fourteen, I'm not sure I would have made good decisions.

I don't regret the boarding school. I learned a lot. But it was hard to be away from all my friends right after losing my mom. And then college. Everyone expected me to do the Ivy League thing, and I did. So that's okay. But then there was the expectation of law school. That's the one I wasn't sure about. Things got confusing."

Her uncle shrugged. "You're taking a break. That's hardly the end of the world."

She sighed. "You sound so rational, but you weren't there. You didn't hear the disappointment in her voice. Or get the look. Oh, she said all the right things, but I knew what she was thinking. I feel horrible but trapped at the same time. I've been living up to all these family expectations when I've never really felt like I'm a part of the family."

Hannah stopped talking and groaned. "Sorry. I'm making a mess of all this."

"No, you're not. Do you think it surprises me to hear you've always felt like an outsider? It shouldn't. Hannah, you were thirteen when we found out you were Billy's daughter. Of course we want to make you feel welcome in the family, but adjustments take time. Just as we were all getting to know each other, you had to leave for school or college. We've never been able to just be a family together and relax. But that doesn't mean we don't care. We all do. We want you to be happy. Even your grandmother."

"I know. Sort of."

He smiled. "You think she wants you to be happy at law school."

"Am I wrong?"

"Probably not, but her opinion is just that. Her

opinion. You're the one who has to live your life. You're the one who has to deal with the consequences."

Hannah thought of the baby growing inside of her. There was one honking big consequence for a decision she'd made.

"I recommend asking for advice from those with relevant experience," he said. "But the ultimate decision must be yours. Once you make it, don't waste time with second-guessing. Just move forward and enjoy yourself."

"Is that your advice?"

"Absolutely. That and eat plenty of ice cream along the way. Oh. Follow your heart. I've followed mine, and I've never regretted it."

"You're talking about Violet, aren't you?"

Ron's features softened. "Yes. She was an amazing woman. I was lucky to have her in my life."

The tale of their love was legendary. Hannah knew she wanted to find that kind of love. One that would last and grow and support both partners.

Was that possible? She instantly thought of Eric, which was silly but probably understandable.

"Have you thought..." She cleared her throat. "I know Violet was the love of your life, but have you thought about maybe finding someone else?"

Ron grinned. "An old man like me?"

She studied his handsome face. There were a few lines, and a couple of gray hairs at the temples, but he was far from old.

"I would be willing to bet a lot of money that you're something of a heartthrob wherever you go," she said. ''If you're still by yourself, it's by choice, not circumstance.''

''I've had my one great love. I'm not saying I believe we only get one chance at being happy. There are degrees of joy and contentment. But what Violet and I had was extraordinary. What are the odds of lightning striking twice?''

''So you don't actually object to loving someone else. You just don't want to settle for second best.''

''Hey, wait a minute. This ice cream session is about you, not me.''

Hannah laughed. ''I know, it's just that I want you to be happy. You're always so great to me, and I appreciate it.''

''I want you to be happy, too.'' He motioned to her empty cup. ''Feel better?''

''Actually, I do. Thank you.''

''Anytime. If May's is closed, give me a call and we'll have some ice cream therapy at my house.''

''It's a deal.''

Hannah's new and improved mental state lasted well into the next morning. She figured the results came from a combination of finally telling her grandmother she was back in town to stay and bonding with her uncle. As much as Ron would probably claim it had been the ice cream, too, she didn't think the sugar stayed in her system that long.

Whatever combination of events conspired to make her hum as she got ready, she was prepared to embrace them fully. She was also going to follow Ron's advice about listening to her heart. It might take her some time to figure out what she wanted to do with her life, but she was excited about the journey.

But the introspection was going to have to wait. She had a doctor's appointment later that morning and she'd missed a call from Eric while she'd been in the shower. Instead of phoning him back and continuing their game of phone tag, she decided to drop in on him on her way to the clinic.

An hour later, dressed in white cropped pants and a light-blue oversize T-shirt, she drove into the hospital parking lot and chose a spot close to the clinic. Then she took the elevator up to Eric's floor.

Jeanne greeted her with a big smile and a wave toward the closed door.

"Hi! For once he's not on the phone, or in a meeting. Let me buzz him. Just a sec." Jeanne pushed a button on her phone. "Hannah's here."

"Send her in."

"You heard the man."

"I did. Thanks." She crossed the foyer to Eric's office door and let herself inside.

"Hannah. This is a nice surprise."

Eric rose and walked around his desk. They met in the middle of his office where he touched her arm and kissed her cheek. She pushed aside a flicker of disappointment. She'd been the one who had wanted things to go more slowly between them. So if he didn't bend her over backward and get her into a lip lock designed to make her toes curl, did she really have anyone to blame but herself?

"You called this morning," she said, explaining her presence. "I was in the neighborhood so I thought

I would return your message by way of a personal visit.''

''Works for me.'' He led her to the sofa in the corner and settled next to her. ''You look great.''

''Thank you.''

He stared at her face. ''Not just the clothes. There's something different.''

She laughed. ''Probably lack of guilt. I don't think I have the personality to make it as a criminal. I've been feeling terrible about keeping my return to town a secret from my grandmother. Yesterday I bit the bullet and went to see her.''

He took her hand in his and gently squeezed her fingers. ''How bad was it?''

''She didn't pull out a shotgun or threaten me, but it was obvious she was disappointed. Still, she knows the truth and that's what matters.''

''I'm sure she'll come around.''

''Maybe. I ran into Uncle Ron right after I left her place and that was great. He made me feel a whole lot better about everything.''

''So that's good.''

''Right.''

''I'd like to change the subject,'' he said.

''Sure.''

''I haven't seen you in a while. How about dinner?''

Heat blossomed inside of her. ''That would be great.''

''I can pick you up at seven.''

''Sounds great.''

She tried not to smile too much as she accepted. It

wouldn't do to look like an idiot. But she couldn't help being happy to be going out with him again.

He released her hand. "So what brought you into my neighborhood?"

"What?"

"You said you dropped by because you were in the neighborhood. I wondered why."

Hannah froze. Every cell in her body went cold, and there was a definite shifting in the rotation of the earth. She was a fool, she told herself. Of course she should have expected the question. It was reasonable. Normal even.

In the second or two before she answered, a thousand thoughts flashed through her mind. The most important were about the decision she faced. She could continue to hedge, or she could tell the truth.

Not much of a choice, she thought. If she and Eric were going to keep seeing each other, she was going to have to come clean. Would there be a better time?

Unlikely, but that didn't change the fact that she didn't want him to know. She didn't want him to judge her or think she was weird or unattractive. She wanted him to keep on liking her and wanting her.

"Hannah? Are you all right?"

"Fine." She swallowed. "I have a routine checkup at the clinic."

"Oh. Makes sense."

She sensed he was about to move on to another topic of conversation. Before he could speak, she threw herself into the deep end and hoped for the best.

"I need to hook up with a doctor as soon as possible."

His dark eyebrows drew together in concern. She pushed on.

"I'm four months pregnant. Routine prenatal care is important for the health of my baby."

She doubted he could have looked more shocked if she'd suddenly morphed into an armadillo. His eyes widened, his mouth dropped open and, worse…he actually slid back a couple of inches on the sofa.

She decided it was probably best for her to keep on talking, so she did.

"I'm going to guess you're wondering why I didn't tell you before. And that's a good question." She glanced down at her lap and saw she'd started twisting her fingers together. She consciously relaxed.

"When we first met up again, I didn't see any reason to mention the pregnancy. I was interested in buying a house and you had one to sell. Talking about my pregnancy seemed inappropriate and irrelevant. I don't walk around introducing myself by saying 'Hi, I'm Hannah, and I'm pregnant.'"

"Good point," he said.

She tried to figure out what he was thinking by the tone of his voice, but she couldn't. He looked a little less shell-shocked, but not especially delighted.

"Our first dinner was fairly casual. I figured I'd get to telling you eventually. Then we had that great kiss and I realized I really liked you."

"So you decided to keep your condition a secret?"

She wasn't sure she liked the words *condition* or *secret* but then, she doubted he liked what she was saying, either.

"Not exactly." She bit her lower lip. "Okay, yes, I was afraid to tell you because I liked what we had going on between us and I didn't want that to change."

He glanced at her stomach. "I would have noticed eventually."

"Granted. Even when I didn't tell you, I knew I was going to have to eventually. So I did. Now you know."

She couldn't tell if he was angry or not. He didn't look annoyed and he wasn't yelling or anything. But he also wasn't smiling.

"Are you mad?" she asked.

"No."

He stood and crossed to the window. She watched the stiffness of his body and the way he stood with his back to her. Okay. Eric wasn't mad, but he wasn't interested, either. She got that message loud and clear.

"I know this is a big deal," she said. "I guess I should have come clean right away. I'm learning that keeping information to myself isn't really working for me. I just hoped..." No point in going there, she told herself.

"I enjoyed our time together," she said as she stood. "You're a great guy. I don't want you to think any of this was about sucking you into a situation you weren't looking for. I wasn't trying to trick you into being the father or anything."

He turned to face her. "I never thought that."

"Good. I just liked being with you, and I didn't want that to end. I still don't want it to end, but if this is all too much for you, I'll understand."

He nodded, but didn't speak. Hannah waited a couple of seconds, then realized he wasn't going to say anything.

The sharp pain in her heart surprised her. Sure she'd hoped he would want to keep seeing her, but if he didn't, she'd figured she would get over him fairly quickly. After all, they'd only been going out for a short period of time.

But the ache in her chest told her otherwise. Apparently, Eric had meant more to her than she'd realized.

Knowing there was nothing else for her to say, she turned and left. The door handle was a bit tricky and as she finally grasped it, she realized there were tears in her eyes.

Get out of here now!

The voice in her head was loud enough to get her feet moving. She hurried past Jeanne and down the hall toward the elevators. She had a few minutes until her appointment. Time to get herself together so she didn't walk into the clinic looking like a wreck.

But while fixing her outsides wouldn't take very long, she had a bad feeling that fixing her insides could be a daunting task.

Eric heard Hannah leave. He stayed where he was, standing at the window looking out but not seeing anything.

Pregnant? She was pregnant?

He didn't know what to think. He flashed over their dinners together and realized she hadn't had anything alcoholic. A clue too subtle for him to catch. Had there been others?

"Eric?"

Jeanne entered the office. "I'm sorry to bother you,

but Hannah just ran out of here and I think she was crying. Is everything okay?''

He looked at his assistant. Jeanne's concern touched him. ''We didn't have a fight.''

''Okay. But something happened.''

Had it? ''She told me she's pregnant. Not by me,'' he added, when Jeanne started talking. ''She's about four months along.''

''Oh, Eric. Can you pick them or what?''

Chapter Eight

Eric sat at his desk after Hannah left. He had a report to read and several dozen e-mails to answer. But despite the waiting work and his usual ability to concentrate, he found himself unable to think about anything but Hannah.

Pregnant? Was it possible?

He frowned as he pictured her body. She sure as hell wasn't showing. He'd spent more than his share of time looking at her. Their last dinner together had ended with a fairly intimate make-out session. If she was pregnant, she didn't look it. At least, not that he could tell.

He swore silently and turned his attention deliberately to his computer. But instead of a blinking cursor, he saw Hannah's face. The wariness in her eyes when she'd told him.

Granted, he didn't know her all that well, but she didn't seem to be the type of woman who slept around. Which meant there'd been a significant relationship in her life a relatively short time ago. So where was he? Why weren't they together? And was the guy the reason she'd left law school and come back to Merlyn County?

He leaned back in his chair. The pregnancy had to have been an accident, he told himself. Hannah was the "get married first" type. So, had the guy disappeared when he'd found out about the baby? Was he dead?

Too many questions, he decided. And he wasn't likely to get any answers himself. He should—

Was she playing him for a fool? Did she want something from him?

Even as those thoughts formed, he dismissed them. Hannah was a Bingham. She sure didn't need him for financial support, and this was a new century. Single mothers were as much a part of mainstream society as married parents. Even here.

So, what was going on?

His need for answers propelled him to his feet. He grabbed his suit jacket as he went.

"I'll be back in about a half hour," he called to Jeanne.

Five minutes later he crossed the glassed-in walkway connecting the hospital with the clinic. The dramatic change in atmosphere caught his attention, as it always did. The hospital was a state-of-the-art health facility where serious people healed serious medical conditions. Long corridors led to gleaming machines.

The clinic, by contrast, was smaller and much more personal. The majority of the staff was female, as were all the patients. The differences could be seen in the softer lighting, the muted colors and the music playing in the background. There were quiet alcoves where families could wait, a day-care center and lots of plants and flowers.

Eric went to the ob/gyn waiting area and glanced around. When he didn't see Hannah in one of the oversize chairs, he spoke with the woman behind the desk.

''I'm looking for Hannah Bingham,'' he said. ''Is she still in with her doctor?''

The woman checked the computer and smiled at him. ''She should be finished in just a couple of minutes. Have a seat and you'll be able to catch her when she comes out.''

''Great. Thanks.''

Eric turned back to the waiting room. It was only then that he noticed how full it was and how most of the women were seriously pregnant. A few were with their husbands or their mothers. Several small children played in a large corner that was carpeted and filled with toys. Eric suddenly felt awkward and out of place.

He sat next to a woman in her late thirties. She rested her paperback book on her massive belly. When he reached for a magazine, she smiled at him.

''Your first?'' she asked.

Hannah pulled her shirt over her head, then slipped into her clogs. Be happy, she told herself. The checkup had gone well, she loved her new doctor and she'd heard the baby's heartbeat. It had been a great visit.

She was happy, she told herself. Really. She was fortunate and positive, and so what if Eric had been upset? Hadn't she expected him to be shocked?

But expecting and living through it weren't exactly the same thing, she admitted to herself as she stepped into the hallway and walked toward the counter where she would confirm her next appointment. Apparently she'd had some secret fantasy about what was going to happen, and when it hadn't, she'd been upset. Crazy. Did she think he would jump for joy, sweep her up in his arms and be thrilled that she was pregnant with another man's child? That didn't even happen on TV.

All things considered, he'd handled the information really well. He hadn't thrown her out of his office, he hadn't called her a slut and he hadn't appeared disgusted or grossed out by the thought of kissing a pregnant woman.

And things hadn't gone that far between them. Which was good because when he called and said he couldn't make their date tomorrow night, she would be okay with that. Yes, he was great and she really liked him, but it wasn't as if she'd fallen in love with him or anything. Getting over him would be a snap.

She gave her name to the clerk and took the appointment card, then stepped out into the waiting room. She was halfway to the main door when she realized someone was calling her name.

She turned and nearly tripped in surprise. "Eric? What are you doing here?"

"Waiting for you."

"I don't understand."

"I can tell. Come on."

He led the way out into the hall. She went along with him because she was too surprised to do anything else. What on earth was going on?

"Is everything okay?" he asked.

"What?"

He glanced at her stomach. "Your appointment. How did it go?"

"Oh. I'm fine and so is the baby. I haven't even gained too much weight, which is good. I've been trying to do a lot of walking."

"So you didn't go to the doctor because something is wrong."

"No. I wanted to hook up with a doctor here. Everything else was just routine."

She clutched her purse with both hands. A part of her wanted to believe his presence meant something really good, but she knew better than to hope.

"So why are you here?" she asked.

"I thought..." He stopped and shrugged. "You dropped a pretty big bomb on me."

"I know. I'm sorry. I've been meaning to say something, but I wasn't sure what or when. At first it seemed really weird to tell you. Then, when we started going out..." She sighed. "I've already said all this. So how mad are you?"

"Not mad. Confused."

She couldn't help smiling. "Didn't your mom ever have that talk with you? Are you still unclear on where babies come from?"

"Very funny."

His expression stayed stern, but she saw the flicker

of amusement in his eyes. The tension in her body eased a little, allowing her to breathe deeply.

"I guess you have a lot of questions," she said. "If you're interested in listening to the answers, I'd be happy to provide them."

"I'd like that." He glanced around at the hallway. "Maybe somewhere other than here."

Nerves appeared in her stomach, but she ignored them and plunged ahead. "Okay, so I was thinking. We already have dinner plans for tonight. We could go ahead with them, but instead of meeting at a restaurant, we could meet at my place. I'd cook. That way it would be more private. I don't mind telling you what happened, but it's not a story I want spread all over town."

"Fair enough. Say seven?"

"I'll be there," she told him.

"Me, too."

She wanted to ask if they were okay, or if they could be okay, but she was too scared. Then Eric took her hand in his.

"Come on. I'll walk you to your car."

"Thanks. That's really sweet."

"I'm a sweet guy. Sexy, too. Ask anyone."

"You and your ego. You don't need anyone else around, do you?"

"Not usually, no."

She laughed, and in that moment she knew everything was going to be just fine.

Despite her earlier reassurance, Hannah still felt nervous as the time for Eric's arrival approached. She found herself pacing the length of the house and smoothing the front of the dress she'd changed into.

"At least I'm getting exercise," she told herself. "Plenty of walking."

On one circuit through the kitchen, she paused to check on the lasagna she'd popped in the oven a short time ago. She'd figured the yummy pasta dish was a good choice for a couple of reasons. First, even if they were still talking when it finished baking, it wouldn't be ruined by just sitting on the counter for a half hour or so. Second, it was one of the few things she knew how to cook.

She'd also made a salad and bought a bottle of Chianti for Eric. But she had changed her mind about the wine and shoved it into the back of the pantry. She didn't want him to think she was trying too hard.

"This would be so much easier if I weren't nervous," she murmured. Of course, wasn't that true for all of life's tense events?

She wanted Eric to understand and accept what had happened and her subsequent choices. In her innermost self, she wanted him to embrace her decision. She figured her odds of the latter happening were pretty close to zero.

She heard a car in the driveway and hurried to the front door. She pulled it open as Eric climbed the steps.

"Hi," he said as he entered the house. "How you feeling?"

She wondered if the question was more than polite chitchat—if it had something to do with him knowing about her pregnancy. But she didn't want to go there so she just said, "Fine."

She led the way to the living room and took a seat on the sofa. He sat in a club chair across from her.

He'd obviously gone home and changed. The tailored dark suit had been replaced by jeans and a short-sleeved shirt. He'd also shaved, which made her notice his face. From there it wasn't much of a stretch to notice his mouth and remember how it had felt against hers. To be honest, a fat, juicy kiss would go a long way to making her feel better, but she wasn't sure Eric would be offering one anytime soon. Not if all the questions in his eyes were anything to go by.

"Would you like something to drink?" she asked.

He shook his head. "I can wait for dinner." He paused and sniffed. "Whatever it is, it smells great."

"Lasagna. One of my roommates in college was Italian. She gave me her mother's secret recipe. I always have fun making it even if I end up dirtying every single pot and pan I own."

She stopped talking when she realized she was within inches of babbling.

"So you're probably wondering what happened," she said.

"Hannah, you don't owe me an explanation."

She considered the statement. "That's true, but I would like you to understand."

"Then I'd like to listen."

She laced her fingers together to keep from twisting them and tried to figure out the best way to start. With Matt? Or had this particular sequence of events been put into play long before she'd met him?

"I told you about going to an all-girls' boarding school," she said.

He nodded.

''The upshot of that,'' she continued, ''is that I didn't date through high school. When I got to college, I found myself sort of behind the curve. I didn't dare tell anyone, which made my first date really scary. I was out with a guy who had every reason to think I knew what I was doing. Instead I was terrified and not that much fun.'' She smiled. ''Let's just say there wasn't a second date.''

''His loss.''

Her heart did a little jig. She wanted to stop and savor the moment, but instead she plunged on.

''Eventually I got better at the whole boy/girl thing. Not great, but better. I had a fairly serious boyfriend my senior year. It came down to us staying together—meaning marriage—or not, and both of us realized we weren't happily-ever-after material. At least not with each other.''

Eric glanced at her midsection, then at her face. ''So he's not…''

''No. He's not the father. My first year of law school I was swamped with work. I had a lot of friends, but no guy. Then last fall I met Matt.''

How to explain, she wondered.

''Matt was…different from the other guys. He made the professors laugh and never seemed worried about tests or studying. That's not to say he didn't do well. He did great. But the problems that plagued the rest of us didn't seem to touch him.''

She thought mentioning that Matt had been a hunk and a half was more than Eric would want to know.

''We were in a study group together, and from the first Matt paid attention to me.''

Eric leaned back in his chair and rested one ankle on his opposite knee. ‘‘So he’s the guy?’’

‘‘Yeah. I thought he was everything I’d ever wanted. When we talked, it was as if he could read my mind about goals and dreams. He was so right for me, it was almost spooky. I—’’ she swallowed ‘‘—I thought I was in love with him. When he asked me to marry him last Christmas, I said yes.’’

Eric’s expression didn’t change, nor did he move. But she sensed him tensing. She quickly went on.

‘‘About three days later I learned that he wasn’t from a wealthy banking family, as he’d always claimed. Over the next week I figured out a lot of what he’d told me had been a lie. I didn’t know why he’d done it. When I confronted him, he eventually came clean about everything.’’

She drew in a deep breath. This was the hard part—the place where she had to admit she’d been a fool.

‘‘He was a brilliant kid from a poor family. He’d been on scholarships since prep school. His goal wasn’t to get a law degree, but to marry a woman with money and live the good life. He recognized the Bingham name and thought I would be a candidate for his plans. As for us being so right for each other, that had just been a game he’d been playing. He’d talked to people who knew me before we ever met and learned as much as he could. He had it all planned out, and I fell for it.’’

‘‘So he broke your heart?’’

‘‘Not exactly,’’ she admitted. ‘‘At first I was stunned. He tried to tell me he still really cared about me, but when I explained how little money there really was, he bugged out. Matt wasn’t interested in a nest egg. He wanted millions. About three days later I found out I was pregnant.''

Eric shook his head. ''Let me guess. He wasn't interested in his responsibility.'' He sounded angry as he spoke.

Hannah wasn't sure she liked her baby being called a responsibility, but she understood his point, because she understood him. If Eric had gotten someone pregnant, he would have taken care of his child for the rest of his life. Loving, or even liking, the mother wouldn't enter into it.

''Matt pretty much freaked when I told him. At first he tried to tell me the baby wasn't his. When I threatened him with a DNA test, he said he knew he was the father but he didn't understand why I was trying to ruin his life.''

She shook her head. ''As if I'd done the whole thing on purpose. But in the end, I was glad he reacted so badly. His craziness helped me figure out what I felt about him and about being pregnant.''

She turned her hands palms up. ''I realized that I was lucky to be free of Matt. That while I'd cared about him, I hadn't been in love with him. Instead I'd been blinded by the show he put on. As for the baby, I was delighted. I wanted to have my child and I knew I could make it as a single mother.''

Eric nodded, as if not surprised by her response. ''Where does Matt fit in now?''

''He doesn't.'' She smiled. ''One advantage of law school is that there are plenty of lawyers hanging around. We had an agreement drawn up. Matt releases all claims to the child, and I don't bother him for child support.''

Eric leaned toward her. "That's not right. He needs to help out."

"Not on my account. I don't want someone like him around my baby. As for making it, I'll be okay. Even with buying the house, I still have enough money from my father to live on. There won't be any extravagant purchases, but I don't have to sweat the day-to-day expenses."

"You left law school because of the pregnancy?" he asked.

"Sort of." She considered the question. "It was the main reason, but I'd been unhappy for a while. I might have decided to study law on my own, but I never had the chance to make that decision. It was very clear to me that this was what the family expected of me. I don't know what I want to do with my life. Once I knew I was pregnant, I decided to take the time to think about my future."

Eric considered all that Hannah had told him. Since learning about the baby, he'd been in shock. He'd figured out there had to have been another guy in her life, but he'd known that guy couldn't be around anymore. Hannah wasn't the kind of woman to play the field. Her explanation had only confirmed his opinion.

His first instinct was to go find that Matt guy and pound him into the ground. What kind of a bastard got a woman pregnant, then walked away from his responsibilities?

Eric knew there were plenty of them around, including his own father.

"You don't sound angry with Matt," he said.

Hannah tucked a loose strand of blond hair behind her ear. "I'm not. I was disappointed for a while, and sad, but now I'm mostly relieved. He's not someone I want in my life."

Made sense, Eric thought. Hannah would be a good mother. Caring, involved. He didn't agree with her decision to leave law school, but he didn't have a trust fund, either.

He glanced around at the warmly decorated living room. "So this is why you wanted to buy a house."

She nodded. "I want my child to have a home and stability."

He or she would have that in spades, Eric told himself. Hannah's love for her child would be in direct contrast to his mother's indifference. She'd lost her heart to the man who had been Eric's father, and when her lover had disappeared, she'd never recovered.

Even if she'd been heartbroken, Hannah would have forced herself to get over it and get on with her life. How much of her backbone came from circumstances and how much of it had she inherited from the Binghams?

"What did your grandmother say when you told her?" he asked.

Hannah winced. "I didn't say anything." She held up a hand before he could speak. "I know. I know. More hiding. I wanted to say something, but she was so disappointed that I'd left law school, I didn't want to make her feel worse." She ducked her head. "Not exactly a well-thought-out plan. She's going to either hear the news from someone else or figure it out for herself eventually."

There was something about the way she sat, as if she were waiting for him to judge her.

"Hannah, this isn't 1950. No one cares if you're pregnant and not married."

She looked at him. "Easy for you to say. You're never going to face the problem. Sure, in a big city, where I wouldn't run into people I know, it wouldn't matter. But here? Don't you think people are going to talk?"

"No, but if *you* do why did you come back?"

"This is my home. I didn't want to go anywhere else. And don't tell me that logic is twisted. I already know it for myself."

"Not twisted. Unusual. You're afraid of what small-town folks will say, yet this is where you decided to hide out."

"I guess the potential for support outweighed my fear."

"Your family may surprise you. In fact, I'm sure they will."

"In a good way, right?"

He smiled. "In a good way."

"Oh, Eric!"

She moved to the coffee table and perched on the edge. She was only a few inches away. The hem of her skirt brushed against his leg.

"I'm sorry," she murmured. She touched the back of his hand with her fingers. "I've behaved so badly about all of this. I really wasn't trying to hide the truth from you." She winced. "Okay, I was, but not for a bad reason. As I told you before, I didn't want things to change. I liked what was happening between us, and I was afraid I would lose that. Can you forgive me?"

Forgive her? He was the one who needed forgiving.

Or a backslap. Here she was, speaking earnestly about her concerns and feelings and all he could think about was how pretty she looked. How big her eyes were and how the shape of her mouth made him want to kiss her. Thoughts of kissing led to other thoughts, like touching her all over. Like wanting her.

He forced his mind away from the erotic images of Hannah and himself…naked.

He was disgusting. What kind of animal would force his carnal desires on a woman in such a delicate condition? It was immoral. It might even be illegal.

He swore silently and vowed he would control himself, regardless of the temptation she presented. There was no way he would violate her trust in him.

"There's nothing to forgive," he said, turning his hand so he could squeeze her fingers. "I want to be your friend in all this."

"I'd like that," she admitted. "I'm feeling pretty alone right now."

"Then you can count on me."

He vowed that he would be there for her. That somehow he would learn to think of her as asexual rather than the lush, desirable woman she was.

"We can be there for each other," he continued. "With my long work hours, I don't have much time for a social life. Jeanne thinks I live for my job, but sometimes it's nice to get away and hang out with someone."

"You're welcome to hang here."

He grinned. "That works. Of course, I'm going to have to bone up on the whole pregnancy/baby thing."

She laughed. "You were always terrific in school.

Why do I know you're going to end up knowing more than me?''

''I doubt that.''

She took his other hand in hers. ''Eric, you have no idea how much your acceptance means to me. Our friendship meant a lot to me before, and I have a feeling it's going to mean even more now. Thank you.''

''My pleasure,'' he said, and meant it.

Her words had caused something to tighten in his chest. He'd never felt the sensation before, and he wasn't sure what it was. But his more pressing concern was the impulse to draw her close and kiss her. He ached to feel her soft mouth against his.

Calling himself an assortment of names, he pushed the need away and stood.

''So when's dinner? I'm starved.''

Chapter Nine

"How did it go?" Jeanne asked the next morning as Eric walked into the office.

He glanced at her in surprise, then looked at his watch. "It's ten after seven."

"I can tell time."

"You never get here before eight."

She sniffed. "What of it? Aren't I allowed to come into work early if I want to?"

Eric set down his briefcase and sat on the corner of her desk. "Thank you," he said.

Her dark eyes narrowed slightly. "For what?"

"Quit being suspicious. For caring enough to come in early."

Jeanne shrugged. "I can't help being curious. Hannah is the first woman to catch your attention in forever. She seems really nice, and I like her. Although

I have to admit the whole pregnancy thing kind of threw me."

"That makes two of us."

Jeanne tapped her desk. "So? How did it go?"

"Good. She explained what happened." He hesitated, not willing to betray a confidence. Hannah hadn't said not to tell anyone about her past, but he would guess she didn't want the whole town talking about it. He sorted through the facts and found the most neutral ones.

"The man responsible is no longer in her life, by mutual decision. She's healthy, happy about the baby, and everything is great."

Jeanne didn't look convinced. "She's going to be a single mother. That's a challenge."

"She was raised by a single mother, so she has a good example. Plus, Hannah is smart and caring. She'll do fine."

"Uh-huh. Kids always do better with a father. Any interest in taking on the role?"

He stood and backed up a couple of paces. "We're still at the friendship stage."

"Really? You could have fooled me. I would have sworn there was more going on than just 'friends.' You can't tell me there isn't a spark."

There was an entire forest fire, but he wasn't about to discuss that with her. Plus, now that he knew Hannah was pregnant, he intended to back off from that sort of thing.

"We're friends," he said firmly. "I plan to keep things that way. Speaking of which, if you get a chance would you please put together a list of books on pregnancy."

Jeanne raised her eyebrows. "I see."

"Don't get too excited. I want to learn what I can, so I can help out. Be there for her. As friends."

"Uh-huh. Sure. I'm convinced. None of this is because you think Hannah is hot."

He picked up his briefcase and headed for his office. "I'm ignoring you."

"That doesn't make me any less right."

Hannah took advantage of the first sun after two days of rain to attack the weeds in her garden. She figured muddy knees were worth the job being easier. Even so, she put a sheet of plastic on the ground and used gloves. In a little less than an hour, she'd made progress through about a quarter of the main bed.

"I have too much energy," she murmured to herself as she plucked the offending weeds. Some of that energy came from the warm, bright morning, but a lot of it grew out of frustration.

Eric hadn't kissed her. Okay, so kissing wasn't required by law, even though it should be after all the trouble she'd gone to while making him dinner. But he hadn't done *anything*. No hug, no hand holding, not even a lustful glance. What was up with that?

Didn't he want her anymore?

Hannah sat up and pulled off her gloves, then pressed her hands to her stomach. The bulge there was getting bigger. She could still hide her condition in clothing, but naked, there was no mistaking what was going on.

Not that she wanted Eric to see her naked. She…

Hannah sighed. Naked would have worked, she thought sadly. Seminaked would have been good, too.

A simple attempt to grab a breast. Something. Anything that would prove he still found her attractive. Because she knew he'd wanted her when they'd kissed in the car and that last time they'd had dinner in her hotel room. She'd felt his arousal.

So what had changed?

Stupid question, she told herself. She was pregnant. *With* another man's child. Talk about a bucket of ice water on the desire front.

But it didn't seem fair. Couldn't she be pregnant *and* a sexual object? Was that too much to ask?

Part of her wondered if he was nervous. Eric was a successful man with a thriving career. Despite working in a hospital, she was going to guess he didn't have much contact with pregnant women. Maybe he didn't know that it was okay to still want her. Maybe he thought her being pregnant meant she wasn't interested in that sort of thing.

"Huh," she said. "Could it be that simple? Do I just have to tell him it's okay to lust after my person and do something about it?"

She grinned at the thought of trying to have *that* conversation. Talk about awkward and *so* not her style. Still, the idea had merit. And if she couldn't tell Eric what she was thinking, maybe she could show him.

Being overtly sexy wasn't something she was good at, but desperate times and all that. A little vamping couldn't hurt.

She began to figure out ways to get his attention. Somewhere between so sexy she would scare him and just plain boring had to be a mix. If she—

The phone rang. Hannah had brought the remote

with her and left it on the front steps. She scrambled to her feet and crossed the square of lawn.

"Hello?"

"Hi. It's Eric."

She clutched the receiver in both hands and tried not to sigh. "I can't believe you're calling in the middle of the day. Don't you have employees to torture and work to assign?"

He chuckled. "One of my meetings got out early and I thought I would give you a call."

"I'm glad you did," she told him. The up side of hearing his voice was the increase in her heart rate. The conversation was practically aerobic.

"How about dinner tonight?" he asked. "It's my turn to treat. You cooked last time."

She thought about her plan to dazzle him with sexy. That would be a whole lot easier in private. Somehow she wasn't really the sashay-in-public type.

"What about take-out?" she asked. "We could eat in here. It's more quiet."

"Sounds like fun. What are you in the mood for?"

"Chinese?"

He hesitated.

"Don't you like Chinese?" she asked.

"Sure. But it can have a lot of sodium."

Hannah held the phone out in front of her and stared at it, then pressed it back against her ear.

"Sodium?" she repeated.

"Sure. Too much salt will make you retain water. I know a great place that doesn't use MSG, so I'll go there. And I can call today and ask about low-salt dishes."

''Sodium?'' she said again before the truth clicked into place. ''You've been reading about pregnancy.''

''Sure. Jeanne picked up a couple of books for me and I read them last night.''

She shook her head. Of course. This was Eric, the overachiever. She'd joked about him learning more about pregnancy than she did, but apparently the laugh was on her.

Still, it was sweet, in a twisted, guy sort of way. ''Low salt is fine with me,'' she said.

''Great. See you about seven.''

''I'll be here.''

Ready to dazzle, she thought as she hung up. She planned to be so sexy—in a low-key way, of course—that Eric wouldn't know what hit him!

Hannah worked her magic as best she could. She curled her shoulder-length hair in fat curlers to give it that artful tousled look. She groomed, she put on makeup and even painted her toes. When the bright red polish was dry, she stared at the color and wondered how long it would be until she couldn't see her feet anymore. Then she studied the contents of her closet.

Nonovert sex appeal was a more complex clothing choice than she would have thought. They were staying in and eating nonsalty Chinese. So a fancy dress was out. Not that she had very many. She didn't want to wear anything that required shoes…not when her bare toes looked so good. Shorts were too casual, but jeans weren't right, either.

She settled on a floral-print skirt with an asymmetrical hem that hiked up on one side. The elastic waist and soft, flowing fabric hid her condition. The matching T-shirt had always been a tad snug. As her pregnancy had progressed, her breast size had increased just enough to make the T-shirt strain across her bust. It also dipped sort of low. She hunted for a push-up bra that would highlight her new assets in the best possible light.

Barefoot, lightly dusted in perfume and swelling above the scooped neck of her shirt, she pronounced herself ready to dazzle. If she had her way, Eric wouldn't know what hit him.

Hannah waited until she heard his car before heading for the door. She greeted him as he climbed the stairs and watched as he got an eyeful of her chest. The poor man nearly stumbled.

She smiled. Everything was going to work out fine.

Or so she thought.

Ninety minutes and one Chinese dinner later, Hannah was ready to stomp her bare foot in frustration. What was going on? Eric had been polite, friendly and annoyingly distant. No matter how she leaned toward him at dinner, he never once looked down her shirt. He'd ignored the light brush of her hand against his arm, her sultry voice as she laughed at his jokes and the way she'd hung on every word.

The latter actions had been sincere and not the least bit thought out. The truth was she *liked* being around Eric, and she liked listening to him talk. But what was up with the rest of it?

Didn't he think she was pretty? Sexy? Appealing? Or had he taken one look at her cleavage and been filled with disgust? What was going on?

Before she could ask—not that she was sure she

had the courage to discuss such a sensitive topic—he pushed back his plate and opened the briefcase he'd brought with him.

Inside were two books on pregnancy and a notepad covered with writing. She glanced at the list.

"What's that?"

"I have some questions about you and the baby." He looked at her. "Is that all right?"

It was if one of them was "Can we get back to the kissing stuff?" but she decided not to say that.

"Sure," she told him. "Only don't expect me to get too technical. I've done all the reading but I still call everything 'stuff' or 'thingie' rather than knowing the correct Latin term."

"Fair enough." He grinned, then turned his attention to the list. "Have you felt the baby move yet?"

She sighed. "No, and I really want to. My doctor swears it's just a matter of time. But as this is my first pregnancy, I'm unlikely to recognize the feelings at first." She held up crossed fingers. "Here's hoping it will be soon."

He went down his list, asking her how she was sleeping, what she was eating, was she taking vitamins. After question five, Hannah lost some of her warm, fuzzy feelings.

"Eric?"

He looked up from his list. "Yes?"

"You're not the boss of me."

"What?"

She tried to smile to show there were no hard feelings, although judging from his wary expression, she thought the smile might have come out more like teeth-baring aggression.

"I'm going to be okay. I know what to eat, how much water to drink, what chemicals to avoid and even that I need to take vitamins. I was in the top fifteen percent of my class when I left law school. I have a brain, and I know how to use it."

He stared at her, then shifted uneasily as his expression turned sheepish. "Sorry. I guess I tried to take charge. Habit."

"You executives. Always feeling the need to lead." She rose and held out her hand. "Come on. Let's go into the living room where you can tell me about your day in the fast-paced world of hospital management."

"Fair enough."

She was pleased when he laced his fingers with hers and walked by her side. Things were looking up. As for his version of "twenty questions" if she looked at it from the right perspective, it was sort of sweet. At least he was concerned and willing to participate—way more than Matt had offered.

They both sat on the sofa. She angled toward him, tucking one leg under her.

"So tell me what's happening at the office," she said. "I'm dying to hear about the outside world."

He took her hand and rubbed his fingers across her knuckles. "Have you considered that need is going to get greater when you're caring for an infant?"

She was so caught up in his touch, she barely heard the question. It took her a second to mentally catch up and produce an answer. "You mean I'll need a grown-up to talk to or I'll go crazy?"

A smile pulled at the corners of his mouth. "I don't think I would have phrased it that way, but yes."

"I know it can be a problem. I'll admit I've thought about how it might get lonely around here. Once I get the garden in shape, I plan to work on the house. I'll keep busy until it's time to give birth. Then when my baby is older, I'll hang with other mothers. When I went in for my checkup I saw a bulletin board listing support groups and play groups."

"What about law school? I know it wasn't your first choice, but you wouldn't be in the top fifteen percent of your class if you hadn't liked some part of it."

"No, I..."

Hannah stopped. She'd planned to tell him that she hadn't liked any of it, but that wasn't true. There were some classes she'd really enjoyed. Various legal professionals offered informal lectures, and she'd attended several. The one that had most interested her had been given by a woman doing legal work for a women's shelter. Hannah remembered thinking how much she would enjoy being able to help in the same way.

"Interesting point," she said at last. "I felt trapped in law school. When I found out about the baby, I only wanted to get away. But there are other options. I shouldn't forget about them." She leaned toward him. "But not everyone wants to rule the world."

"I'm not interested in the world," he told her. "Just a Fortune 500 corporation."

"That's a big dream."

"I can handle it."

She didn't doubt that, but she wondered what the price would be. CEOs often sacrificed hours at home for hours on the job. How could a woman be first in Eric's life if the job mattered more?

"What about balance?" she asked. "You have to have other goals. Personal ones."

He shrugged. "Sure. I guess. Eventually."

Not exactly the endorsement she was looking for. "What about finding your soul mate? Don't you want to be a part of something?"

As she asked the question, she noticed his gaze had dipped below her face to the vicinity of her chest. Suddenly getting the answer didn't seem all that important. Not when he'd finally remembered she was a woman.

She breathed his name, then leaned toward him. He matched her movements, pressing close and putting his hands on her shoulders.

It was perfect…better than perfect. It was exciting and hot and all this before they'd even kissed! She couldn't wait for the real thing.

But just before she felt the first whisper of contact, he abruptly pulled away and sprang to his feet.

"Look at the time," he said with forced cheer. "Wow. And I have an early meeting in the morning."

She stared at him. "You're leaving? It's barely eight."

"I know, but I have to prepare, and you need your rest."

"Not that much."

Her words had no impact—he was already edging toward the door.

Not sure what was going on, how to fix it or even what to say, Hannah reluctantly followed. Any hope she'd had of a good-night kiss was dashed as he bolted for freedom. Seconds later she heard the sound of his car engine as he sped away.

Something was very wrong, she thought as she leaned against her closed front door. Very wrong. And she was determined to find out what.

Eric knew he'd somehow landed in hell. Or he was being punished for an unknown offense. Those were the only two possible explanations for the last week of intense suffering.

No matter how he tried, he couldn't stop wanting Hannah. Even though it was wrong. Even though it made him completely twisted and sick, he couldn't stop thinking about her. He consoled himself with the realization that he didn't just want her in bed. While the thought of making love with her got his temperature climbing, his body thrumming and his crotch as hard as granite, he also wanted to spend nonsexual time with her.

He liked being around her, talking with her, listening to her talk. He liked the sound of her laughter, the way she walked, her smile. It was just that close proximity brought his animal nature to the forefront, which made him think about sex, which made him a seriously sick puppy.

It also made him uncomfortable. He'd almost given up on ever getting any sleep. Despite leaving his teens behind nearly a decade before, he'd started having erotic dreams. But instead of faceless female bodies, the star of these nighttime fantasies was one Hannah Bingham.

So he knew he was in hell or going to hell or both.

And no matter what his pain level, he couldn't seem to stop spending time with her. Like today.

He stood in the middle of Baby World and wondered how it was possible for something so small to need so much.

''This can't all be for one baby,'' he told Hannah.

She opened her purse and handed him a detailed list. ''I copied this from one of my pregnancy books. This is just the basics of what a newborn needs. Oh, there's a second page,'' she added helpfully.

He scanned the list and felt his panic level rise. Just the part about clothes confused the hell out of him. ''What's a romper and how is it different from a stretchy with feet?''

''You're asking me? This is my first time, too.'' She led the way farther into the bowels of the store. ''I'm guessing all the clothes will be labeled. Right now I'm more concerned about furniture. If I find a crib and matching changing table that have to be special ordered, I want to make sure they get here in time.''

''Yeah, you don't want the kid sleeping on the floor.''

She gave him a grin over her shoulder and kept on moving.

They passed stacks of blankets, acres of lamps and accessories that looked like something out of a science fiction movie. When he saw a display of baby clothes, he stopped to look.

''Furniture,'' Hannah said firmly.

''Wait a second. These aren't all fuzzy, pink and blue things.'' He picked up a miniature leather motorcycle jacket. ''This is kind of cool.''

"You are such a guy," Hannah told him as she took the jacket and hung it back on the rack.

"Oh, look. A baseball uniform." He held up the set and frowned. No way it should be this small, he thought, taking in the tiny shirt and matching pants.

"They made a mistake with this one," he told her. "It shrank."

Hannah looked at the tag. "It says six to nine months."

Eric nearly dropped the hanger. "The kid's only going to be this small after *nine* months? Jeez. What size is it when it's born?"

Hannah flipped through the clothes on the rack and held up a duck-covered sleeping thing that was barely larger than his hand.

"This one is for a newborn," she told him.

He put the baseball outfit back and tucked his hands behind his back. "No way. Babies need to be bigger. It's a kid, not a Chihuahua puppy."

She laughed. "Speaking as the person who has to give birth to this child, small is good. Did you expect him or her to pop out fully grown?"

"No, but it should be big enough to be, you know. Sturdy."

"Sturdy? Sorry. Babies are helpless and need to be cared for."

"Sure. The caring part is okay, but they're too small. We need to talk to someone."

"Who would you suggest?"

He chuckled. "Someone in management."

"I'll write a letter. Come on. We can coo over the clothes later. I want to pick out some furniture."

Eric followed her toward the rear of the store. "I wasn't cooing."

"If you say so."

"I want that to be clear. I'm not the kind of guy who coos. Ever. I have a reputation."

"So I've heard." She paused beside a crib. "What's going to happen when word gets out that you were spotted here?"

People would assume he'd lost his mind, he told himself. Maybe they would be right. After all, he had rules about not getting involved. For reasons he hadn't figured out, he never confirmed that Hannah was only into their relationship for the good times and not anything serious. Now they'd become friends, and he wasn't sure how to have the conversation.

Not that it was an issue. He and Hannah weren't going to be intimate. Not while she was pregnant. And her due date was months away. He didn't have to sweat that. Just his growing attraction to her and how great she looked in her dress.

He glanced at the curve of her shoulder and the way the hem of her dress flirted with her thighs. Her skin was smooth and tanned from her hours in the garden. She was well toned, too. Now that he knew about the baby, he could detect a slight rounding to her stomach, but that only added to her allure. She was lush…in all the right places.

His thoughts had a predictable response, so he did his best to ignore them. Instead he walked around the display of cribs and recalled what the baby books he'd read had said was important.

"The railings have to be close together," he said. "So the kid can't stick its head through."

She looked at him and raised her eyebrows. "Do we have to have the 'I can read' conversation again?"

"Maybe."

She laughed. "Fair enough. We'll confirm with the salesperson that all the cribs we like are up to code, or whatever it's called."

Eric rubbed the finish of a walnut crib. "What kind of wood are you looking for? Have you picked colors?"

"I'm thinking lighter stain rather than darker. It's more neutral."

"So you don't want something painted."

"I don't think so. What about you?"

"I prefer the stain. This maple's nice."

She walked over to the crib and studied it. "You're right. I suppose this would be easier if I'd picked the colors for the room. The thing is I'm still caught up in the gender debate."

He put his arm around her and ignored the soft feel of her body next to his.

"I hate to break this to you, kid, but you don't get to decide. The gender has already been picked."

She glared at him. "I know that. My point was do I want to know if I'm having a girl or a boy."

"You're kidding? They can tell?"

"Usually. In an ultrasound. That is if the baby's positioned right."

He liked that. "Very cool."

She looked at him. "I'm having one next week. Want to come?"

He hesitated. Imagining Hannah naked was one thing, but actually seeing it. Not that he didn't want to, but not in a doctor's office. There were—

She poked him in the side. ''Stop panicking. They put gel on my tummy and use a wand to check things out. Except for my midsection, I'm completely dressed.''

Bummer. ''Sure. I'll go. I would like to see the ultrasound pictures.''

''Me, too. I understand now they can give you a snapshot to take with you. That would be very exciting.''

''We'll have to get a little frame for the picture.''

She linked arms with him and leaned close. ''Great idea.''

''I'm known for my ideas.''

''Any others you want to share?''

He shook his head. The only images floating around in his head would get him in a lot of trouble. Better to play it safe and lie.

Chapter Ten

Once again Eric found himself in the clinic's waiting room, but this time he felt less out of place. Hannah sat next to him, squirming slightly.

"Tell me they're going to call us soon," she whispered.

He glanced at his watch. "The receptionist said two or three minutes. It's been less than one."

Hannah shifted again. "I really have to go. I'd heard that timing the full bladder for the ultrasound was really tough, but tough doesn't begin to describe it."

He took her hand in his. "Try not to think about it."

She glared at him. "You try sitting here with an elephant pressing on your bladder after drinking about four thousand glasses of water and we'll see how much you can't think about it."

"When did you get cranky?"

"About ten minutes ago." She sighed. "I should be nicer to you. After all, you took time off work to come over here. And I really appreciate that. I just wish they'd let me go to the bathroom."

A door opened and a nurse called Hannah's name. She sprang to her feet and hurried toward the examination rooms. Eric practically had to sprint to keep up with her.

The nurse smiled. "The need to pee, huh?"

"In spades."

"Don't worry. Once you're on the table, everything goes quickly. In here." She motioned to a small room filled with equipment. "There's a gown on the chair."

Eric waited until the nurse left, then grabbed the door handle. "I'll wait out here while you change," he said. "Call me when you're ready."

"Okay."

Hannah stepped inside, and he closed the door behind her.

The books he'd been reading explained what was going to happen during the ultrasound, but he couldn't imagine seeing a visual image of the baby. Would they be able to distinguish different parts of the body? Were there—

"Eric?"

He turned and saw his sister walking down the hallway. She stopped in front of him.

"I thought that was you. What on earth are you doing here?"

He motioned to the door behind him. "Helping out a friend. She's having an ultrasound and I—"

CeCe's eyes widened. "You didn't get some girl pregnant, did you?"

He laughed. "Not even close. Jeez, give me a little credit."

"I guess I'd better. I was going to say I didn't know your relationship with Hannah had progressed to the point where she *could* get pregnant."

"I don't kiss and tell."

CeCe shook her head. "Actually, you told me the two of you were kissing."

"Okay. I don't do other stuff and tell."

"Good thing, because I'm your sister and I have to say hearing about your sex life would be really creepy."

She tucked a loose strand of dark hair behind her ear. Eric studied her, noting the dark shadows under her eyes and the lines of strain around her mouth.

"What's up?" he asked.

"Nothing." CeCe leaned against the wall and sighed. Then she lowered her voice. "We delivered a stillborn this morning. The mother was strung-out on drugs, so the baby would have had tons of problems, but man, I hate it when that happens." She rubbed her temples. "We all tried to save the baby. There wasn't anything we could do."

He put his arm around her. "I'm sorry."

"Thanks." She looked at him. "I try not to take the losses personally, but I can't seem to help myself."

"That's what makes you so good at your job."

"You're being sweet to me. I appreciate that."

Before she could say anything else, her beeper went off. Eric gave her a quick hug then released her.

CeCe read the display as she hurried back the way she'd come.

No doubt another woman had gone into labor and needed her midwife at hand. His sister had always loved her work. He couldn't remember the number of cards, letters and gifts of thanks she'd received over the years. A large percentage of the school-age population in town had been delivered by CeCe.

He knew that losing a baby always hit her hard. She—

Eric froze. A baby had died. Yes, the mother had been on drugs, but that didn't mean that other children couldn't be at risk.

He thought about Hannah and her happiness about her pregnancy. Suddenly, fiercely, he wanted to figure out how to keep her and her child safe. Nothing could ever happen to them.

Before he could figure out a plan, or even know what was wrong, the door opened and Hannah stuck her head out.

"I'm ready. Do you see the technician? I swear, I'm going to lose it right here and that's going to be some mess to clean up."

He didn't want Hannah to suspect anything was wrong, so he forced himself to smile. "Want me to ask for a porta-potty?"

"Not a bad idea." She sighed. "Maybe lying down would be better. What do you think?"

Until that second, he hadn't really noticed that she'd changed her clothes, but now he realized she was in a hospital gown and very little else. Her legs were bare, as were her arms. As she walked toward the table, he saw the gown was open. He could see her back, her pale-pink panties and sexy thighs that cried out to be touched.

His arousal was as instant and strong as an earthquake. Calling himself a pervert didn't help. Nor did looking away. The image of her body had burned itself onto his brain. If he closed his eyes, the picture only got more vivid.

"Morning," a young woman said as she breezed into the room. "Okay, let's get this over with so you can run to the bathroom."

"Please," Hannah breathed as she scrambled onto the table.

Eric moved forward to help her. He held out his arm for her to push against. She shifted and pushed up, but as she moved, the edge of the hospital gown got caught. Hannah kept going and it didn't. The sudden gaping of the neckline gave him a clear view of bare, full breasts and tight nipples. His knees nearly went weak.

This was so wrong, he told himself. He had no right to look, and he sure as hell wasn't supposed to get turned on by what he'd seen. So what if Hannah was beautiful and sexy and... He clenched his teeth together and vowed to act like a grown-up, not some horny adolescent boy. The problem was, the more he tried *not* to think about her curves, the more they filled his mind.

The technician introduced herself as Sandra.

"Let me drape this across your legs," the woman said as she unfolded a patterned drape over Hannah's lower half. "Then we'll roll up your gown."

When the fabric was nestled below Hannah's breasts, Sandra picked up a bottle of gel.

"Don't worry. We keep it nice and toasty." Sandra grinned. "We don't want the shock of something cold to cause you to lose control."

"I appreciate that." Hannah drew in a breath as she glanced at Eric. "Ready?"

"Sure."

He didn't know what to expect as he turned toward the screen. The image was just a jumble of lines and shaded areas. Sandra shifted the wand, and suddenly he could see a curve of what looked like a spine, and a head.

The truth slammed into him like a hundred-mile-an-hour fast ball. That was a baby. Hannah's baby.

Hannah stared at the picture and wanted to cry with happiness. Her throat tightened and her eyes burned. But she refused to give in to tears because she didn't want to miss a moment.

"Look's good," Sandra said. "Here's the head. That's easy to see. Arms, legs." She smiled. "Your little one seems to be sleeping."

Hannah wanted to put a protective hand over her stomach or tell everyone to be quiet, which was crazy. She felt excited, thrilled and just a little scared at the thought of being solely responsible for the life growing inside of her.

Without thinking, she turned to Eric. She held out her hand at the exact second he reached for it. Their fingers laced together.

Sandra continued the examination, pointing out the organs and explaining that the baby's size was exactly right for that many weeks along. Finally she let them listen to the heartbeat.

The steady sound filled Hannah with contentment.

Her baby, she thought happily. He or she was growing just fine. They were going to be a very happy family together.

And just for that moment, even though she knew it was foolish, she allowed herself to pretend that she wasn't in this alone. That Eric was along, not because he was a friend, but because he was something more. Someone who mattered and wanted to be a part of things. Foolish dreams, she told herself. But harmless. As long as she didn't let herself forget that it was all just pretend.

''How are you feeling?'' Eric asked as he walked into her house that evening after work.

''I told you, I'm great.'' Hannah patted her stomach. ''But I never want to drink that much water at one time ever again. Talk about painful.''

He chuckled. ''When you got off the table, you actually ran out of the room. Impressive. I've never seen a pregnant woman sprint before.''

''It's going to get a lot more humorous as I get bigger.''

She thought about mentioning that there was another way to take an ultrasound, one that didn't involve her drinking until she was about to burst. But she wasn't sure Eric wanted to discuss that more intimate procedure. Nor would she be comfortable having him in the room while it was happening.

''You're going to have to decide about knowing the baby's gender,'' he said as he shut the front door and followed her into the kitchen.

''I guess. I just don't know if I want to be told in advance.''

"It's going to be a boy," he said confidently as he leaned against the counter.

"Oh, sure, because that would be more interesting for you." She sighed. "Still, it was very exciting to see the baby like that. Wasn't the heartbeat cool?"

"Yeah. All the new technology makes everything more immediate." He smiled at her. "You're going to be a mom."

"Sometimes that thought terrifies me."

"It shouldn't. You'll do a great job."

"Maybe. I want to, of course. My mother was amazing, so I have her example to follow. It's nice to have that kind of role model in my background. But sometimes, when I think about the responsibility, I worry about all the places I could mess up."

He touched her cheek. "No one expects perfection. In fact, I think it would be scary for the kid."

"I hope you're right."

"Aren't I always?"

She laughed. "Eric, you never lack for self-confidence."

"What's the point in that?"

He spoke lightly, but there was something dark in his eyes. Something dark and sensual that made her lean toward him. His long fingers caressed her cheek. The wanting that was always a problem when he was around exploded into life, taking over her body and making her weak with need.

She covered his hand with hers and sighed. Expectation filled her as he lowered his gaze to her mouth. He was going to kiss her. She could feel it. And if the kissing led somewhere else, she was more than ready. Past ready. She was approaching desperate.

But instead of brushing his mouth against hers, he dropped his hand to his side and took a step back.

"You might as well give in and paint the room blue," he said. "You're going to have a boy and all the yellow paint in the world isn't going to change that."

She recognized the teasing challenge and knew that she was supposed to take him on, arguing for a girl. She knew that she was also supposed to ignore the tension between them, the almost kiss and the way she felt. But she was tired of ignoring and pretending it didn't matter when it did…very much. She wanted to know what was going on and there was only one way to find out.

Ask.

She swallowed her fear and blurted out, "Is it the pregnancy? Because I'm carrying another man's child? Or is it the whole body change thing? Is that disgusting?"

Eric stared at her. "What are you talking about?"

"Us. This." She motioned to him and then the room. "We're spending time together, which I enjoy, but everything is different. Before you knew about the baby, we were dating. Now I don't know what we're doing. It's not dating. For some reason you've put a halt to the physical side of the relationship, and I want to know why. If you're just interested in being friends, I can live with that. What I can't stand is not knowing what's going on."

His dark gaze never left her face. One corner of his mouth twisted slightly. "I wasn't sure you'd noticed."

''How could I not? Two weeks ago we were making out on my sofa. Now if I get too close you bolt.''

He shoved his hands into his slacks front pockets. ''I want to be your friend,'' he told her. ''I want to be here for you. I enjoy spending time with you.''

All nice, but *so* not the point. ''And?'' she prompted.

''I backed off on the rest of it because I had to.''

She felt the first twinge of pain but was determined to ignore it. ''Okay. Why?''

''Because. I had to. We can't make love *now.*''

Her thoughts ranged from him finding her hideous to that weird, twisted place some men go—that a mother could no longer be sexy.

''Why?'' she asked.

He looked at her as if she'd just asked him to stick his hand in boiling water. ''You're pregnant.''

''I actually know that.''

''I don't want to hurt you or the baby.''

She blinked. No way. ''That's it?''

''Of course. I was afraid something bad would happen.'' His expression turned sheepish. ''Plus I wasn't sure if it was okay to be attracted to a pregnant woman. Not that you're not gorgeous and sexy,'' he added hastily. ''You are. You're sexy as hell, and it drives me crazy. But I figured I shouldn't go there, and it's been killing me.''

The pain faded as hope and excitement took its place. ''In what way?'' she asked as she moved closer.

He groaned. ''The shorter answer is how it hasn't been. Just being around you is torture. Today, at the clinic. You were having a *medical* procedure and all I could think about was touching you everywhere.''

Shivers of anticipation climbed up her spine. ''I had no idea.''

He nodded. ''I felt like such a jerk. When you climbed onto the table, your gown fell open and I could see...'' He turned away. ''I saw your breasts. I know. I'm a disgusting animal.''

He was too sweet for words. And interested in her. It was a combination designed to steal her heart.

''Eric,'' she whispered, as she put her hand on his arm. ''I'm glad you find me sexy. For one thing it makes me feel really good about how I look, which as I expand on a daily basis is pretty thrilling. For another, I don't want to be the only one lying awake nights thinking about us being together.''

She'd never been this forward with a man before, but then she'd never felt as comfortable as she did around him. So while speaking the words made her a little nervous, there wasn't any out-and-out terror. Especially when he turned back to face her and she saw the heat in his eyes.

''I want you,'' he breathed. ''All the time. It's driving me crazy.''

''So what's stopping you from taking what you want?'' she asked softly.

He groaned low in his throat, then reached for her. As his arms came around her body, she settled her hands on his broad shoulders and clung to him. Their mouths met in a deep, hot kiss that spoke of passion and desire, of need and wanting and too much time spent waiting.

His tongue brushed against hers, making her

squirm closer, wanting to be part of him. He tasted sweet and masculine, his lips were firm, yet gentle. Everywhere their bodies touched, heat sparked and flared and made her start to melt. Between her thighs, she felt dampness. Her breasts ached in anticipation. She wanted more. She wanted it all. She wanted their lovemaking to last forever.

He tilted his head and deepened the kiss. At the same time, he ran his hands up and down her back. Her dress, a thin cotton sundress with a built-in bra, seemed like an impenetrable barrier. She wanted him to tug down the zipper and bare her to his gaze. She wanted to feel his skin against hers. She wanted him inside of her, making her writhe, making her scream.

The intensity of her response stunned her. Matt had only been her second lover, and while their time together had been pleasant, she didn't remember ever feeling this...desperate.

She reached down to tug on the knot of Eric's tie. Even as she pulled the length of silk free and tried to go to work on his shirt buttons, he kissed his way from her mouth to her jaw, then to her ear.

The delicious grating of his teeth on her earlobe made her shudder. She couldn't think, couldn't breathe, couldn't do anything but stand there lost in the sensation of the rough caress, the feel of his breath on her neck, and know that it was all only going to get better.

When he licked the sensitive skin below her ear, she groaned. Every cell in her body was on alert. Her skin felt hot and tight and hungry.

"Walk," he whispered in her ear.

She didn't understand what he was saying, nor did

she want to. This wasn't the time for talk. She only wanted him to *do.*

"Walk," he repeated, pushing her gently toward the living room. "Bedroom. Bed. Naked."

The last two words sank in and she started moving. She took his hand and led the way to the opposite side of the house. But in the doorway to her bedroom he pulled her close, her back nestling against his front. His hands came around to cup her breasts while she felt him pressing into her.

He was already hard and, if his breathing was anything to go by, more than ready. His arousal delighted her. She wanted him to need as much as she did. She wanted this to be for both of them.

She wanted a lot of things, but as he took the weight of her breasts in the palms of his hands and brushed his thumbs against her tight nipples, she didn't care about any of that, or anything other than that he never, ever stop.

He brushed against the tight tips with his thumbs, then used his forefingers. He circled around the edge of the nipple, rubbed the whole breast, then returned to the center.

Pleasure poured through her. In the first couple of months of her pregnancy, her breasts had been sensitive to the point of pain. But that had faded, and now his gentle touch made her moan.

She pushed her chest into his hands, arching her back and resting her head on his shoulder. He took advantage of the position to bend down and press an openmouthed kiss against her bare skin.

The combination of him licking and kissing her neck while touching her breasts was nearly too much for her to experience and still stay standing. She thought about suggesting they move toward the bed, but before she could speak, he slipped one of his hands lower. Across her stomach to her hip, where he paused and started pulling up her skirt.

Inch by inch the fabric rose. First to knee, then to thigh. Finally he had it all bunched in his hand. He released the fabric, but only after slipping under it. He pressed against the swell of her bare tummy before moving down to her bikini panties.

From there it was a short journey past elastic, lace and silk to the waiting wetness between her legs. Even as he continued to rub her breasts and nipples and kiss her neck, he slid between protective curls and found that one place of pleasure.

That he found it on the first try impressed her. That he knew what to do when he did made her suck in her breath and nearly collapse.

Not too rough, not to fast, he moved like a man with all the time in the world and the motivation to make that time be about her desires. He circled the one small spot, gently caressing it. First one finger, then two. He moved a little faster, exciting her, then slower, making her anticipate.

She reached up one hand to touch his head. She wanted to turn toward him so they could kiss, but she didn't want him to stop what he was doing. She wanted to touch *him,* to take off her clothes, to be on the bed, but again, all of that would require him to stop his delicious torture.

He abandoned the spot to dip inside. The deep stroking made her muscles clench. She was so wet. She could feel it in the slickness as he moved. Parting her legs, she pulsed her hips, wanting more. Wanting it all.

He returned to that one place and rubbed a little harder. His speed increased, as well, and soon there was nothing for her to do but give in. Her mind went blank, her body tensed, she pressed her hand against his forearm and silently begged him not to change anything.

Surrender became inevitable. Standing there in the entrance to her bedroom, she felt the release surge, then spill over, rippling through her as wave upon wave of pleasure made her muscles contract and relax in a rhythm as old as the tide.

When she'd finished, he pulled his hand out of her panties and released her breasts, then turned her toward him and kissed her. Strong arms wrapped around her, pulling her close. She pressed against him, sated, yet oddly still aroused.

His need pressed into her belly. She rubbed against it, making him groan.

He pulled back slightly. "Where the hell is the zipper on this damn dress?" he demanded.

Hannah opened her eyes and stared at him. She smiled, then giggled, then laughed. "You don't know?"

Frustration and need darkened his eyes. "I haven't a clue. I've been subtly trying to find it since we started in the kitchen. I feel like a teenager on his first make-out session."

She touched his mouth. "Hardly that. If we'd been teenagers, I would never have let you get to third base."

He smiled. "You liked me on third base."

"Oh, yeah."

"Good." He kissed her. "I liked being there. But right now I'd like to get you naked. Any hints would be appreciated."

She turned so her left side faced him, then raised her arm. He stared at the zipper tab.

"Well, I'll be damned. That's tricky."

He reached for the zipper and pushed her toward the bed at the same time. When her dress hit the floor, she was already beside the mattress.

Any self-consciousness she might have had about her pregnancy showing vanished when she saw Eric's appreciation as he looked at her body. His gaze lingered on her full breasts. She saw his arousal pulse as he reached out and touched her nipple.

While she pulled off her panties and slid onto the bed, he tugged at his clothing. Soon he was naked and next to her. Then they were kissing.

As he claimed her mouth, he touched her everywhere. His strong, sure hands caressed her breasts, her stomach, then her legs. She parted her thighs for him, already anticipating his touch there. Despite her earlier release, she found herself wanting him again.

This time he rubbed her with his thumb while dipping his fingers inside. When she was tense and breathing hard, he eased between her legs and slowly entered her.

He was large and thick and he stretched her delightfully. Bracing himself on his arms, he supported his weight, gazing down at her as he filled her over and over again. With each movement, her body clenched around him. Pleasure built. She was so close, so very close.

Back and forth, back and forth. Finally he shifted so that he was sitting on his heels, still inside of her but now able to reach between their bodies. He stretched out one arm so he could touch her breasts and brought his other hand between their bodies. He touched that one hypersensitive center.

The combination was more than enough to send her flying. Contractions seized her body. Once they started, she didn't want them to ever stop.

While she was still caught up in her own release, she was vaguely aware of Eric shifting against her, braced over her, pumping in and out, faster and faster until he groaned her name and was still. Then he collapsed next to her, pulling her with him, so they were still connected but on their sides.

As she slowly surfaced and was able to think consciously, she realized that even in the throes of passion, he'd been as careful not to put too much of his weight on her as he'd been to please her. Which made Eric a pretty amazing guy. She wasn't sure how she'd gotten so lucky, but she wasn't going to question her good fortune.

Eric woke sometime just after five in the morning. He hadn't planned to spend the night, but after he and Hannah had made love twice more, he'd been more than happy to stay in her bed.

Now his eyes popped open in the semidarkness and a sense of horror swept through him.

What the hell had he done?

He glanced at Hannah and knew if he'd hurt her or the baby, he would never forgive himself. Sure, all the books said lovemaking was perfectly safe for both mother and child. But he knew what those authors were talking about. Gentle bonding every few days. Not passionate, intense, erotic experiences that made the mother have several climaxes.

Panic filled him. He'd acted without thinking and now they were all going to pay the price.

Not knowing what else to do, he climbed out of bed and reached for his clothes. He only knew one person who would have all the answers. Even if the truth about him made her hate him for the rest of his life.

•

Chapter Eleven

The morning was still cold and dark when Eric pulled up in CeCe's driveway. He sat in his car for several minutes while he considered waiting until at least 6:00 a.m. before pounding on her door. But the thought of sitting out there seemed impossible. Finally he reached for his cell phone and punched in a number.

It was answered after three rings. A groggy female voice said, "Hello?"

"Hey, sorry to wake you. It's me."

He heard movement, as if his sister was turning over in bed, or sitting up. "Eric? Is that you? What's going on? It's—" there was a low groan "—tell me it's *not* quarter after five in the morning."

"My watch says 5:16."

"Oh, well then. That makes it better. So why are

you calling me?'' Her faintly annoyed tone changed to concern. ''Is something wrong? Are you hurt? Were you in an accident?''

''No. Not exactly. Look. I need to talk to you. Can you let me in?''

There was a pause. ''Let you *in?* You're *here?*''

''Sitting in your driveway.''

''Great. Give me a couple of seconds.''

There was a click as she hung up.

He saw lights go on in the small house. As he walked to the front door, he heard the lock turn. When he went inside, CeCe had already headed for the kitchen. Water ran as she filled the coffeepot.

''I was trying to cut back on caffeine,'' she grumbled when he entered the room. ''Getting a predawn wake-up call isn't going to help my cause.''

He hovered in the doorway and shoved his hands into his slacks pockets, not sure what he should say. In his initial panic, his sister had seemed like the only person he could talk to. Now that he was here, he didn't know how to start or what to explain.

CeCe finished with the coffeemaker and hit the switch. Then she collapsed onto a kitchen chair and ran her fingers through her dark hair.

''Talk,'' she demanded. ''And this had better be good.''

Eric took a step toward the table, stopped and sucked in a breath. Okay, what he wanted to know was had he hurt either Hannah or the baby.

The baby. He closed his eyes, trying not to see the tiny new life he'd viewed on the ultrasound image. Her child had been so small and perfect. An innocent. He was—

"Eric!"

He opened his eyes and saw his sister staring at him. "What?" she asked. "Tell me what's going on." She narrowed her gaze. "You look like you didn't sleep at all. Did you work all night? Is there some crisis at the hospital? Because news about that could have waited."

He rubbed his hand against the stubble on his chin. He hadn't showered or shaved. When he'd awakened, he'd simply panicked.

"It's not work," he told her as he pulled out the chair opposite hers. "It's...personal."

He sat down and wished the coffee would hurry. Already the scent filled the kitchen, but there was barely enough in the pot to fill one cup, and he didn't think CeCe would take kindly to him claiming it for himself.

"I just didn't know who else to talk to."

Her dark gaze settled on his face. "Okay. I'm awake, and I'm prepared to listen. What's up?"

The concern in her voice made him feel better. In the past he'd always known that, whatever happened, he could count on his sister. He just hoped she didn't turn her back on him this time, when she found out that he'd—

"Stop thinking about it and tell me!" she yelled. "Just spit it out."

"Hannah is pregnant, and I spent the night with her."

CeCe looked at him for several seconds. She shook her head, then rested both elbows on the table and dropped her head to her hands. "Want to run that one by me again?"

"I told you I've been seeing Hannah Bingham."

"Sure. I warned you that she was trouble. But did you listen? No."

"Do you want to tell this story or should I?"

She glanced at him through her mussed bangs and sighed. "Go ahead. I'll be quiet and listen."

He explained about Hannah's return to town and how she'd bought the house from the hospital. "We started seeing each other. Things were progressing well, then she told me she was pregnant."

"With some other guy's kid."

"Right."

CeCe straightened, then glanced at the coffeepot. "At last," she breathed as she rose. "So what's the problem? Are you concerned about the responsibility? Because I have to say, taking on a ready-made family could be a challenge. Not that it wouldn't be good for you. Despite not having a father in your life I think you'd do a good job. It's just that you have these goals and would a family—"

"CeCe?"

"What?"

"Stop talking."

She poured them each a mug of coffee. "Fine. You talk, I'll listen."

"Thanks." But he waited until she returned with the coffee before continuing.

"At first I was shocked about her being pregnant. Plus, I didn't want to do anything to compromise her health, so I backed off."

His sister winced. "Eric, if we're going to talk about you having sex, I'm going to need the rest of that pot first."

"I'm serious. I didn't know if it was okay for us to be intimate."

"It's fine," she said with a wave of her hand. "Actually it's pretty sweet that you think she's attractive. How far along is she?"

"Four months and she *is* attractive, but that's not the point."

He stood and paced the length of the kitchen. "You don't understand. I know it's all right for couples to have marital relations."

CeCe snorted. "Since when did you ever call sex that? Just say 'do it.' You'll be more comfortable."

"This isn't funny." He spun to face her. "Last night, when we were together..." He swallowed. "I'm afraid it was too much. That I hurt her or the baby." His chest tightened. "What if something bad happened? I could never forgive myself. Hannah loves this baby. If I..."

He couldn't speak. Instead he faced the cabinets and clutched the counter with both hands. If he'd done anything—there was no punishment powerful enough.

He heard his sister's chair scrape against the floor, then the sound of her footsteps. Her arm wrapped around his waist.

"I'm sorry I'm not taking this seriously," she said quietly. "Obviously, you're really worried. But don't be."

"You don't know what happened."

"I have a fair idea. Can I assume you stayed within the parameters of normal as far as position? You on top or her on top?"

He didn't want to be talking about this with her, but he forced himself to nod.

"Okay." She leaned her head against his arm. "And it was probably good for both of you?"

"Yes. All three times."

CeCe groaned. "That does it. The next guy in my life is going to be young enough to cause a scandal. All that energy and surging hormones."

Eric winced. "Sis, could you not say that?"

"Sorry."

She grabbed him by the arms and turned him until he faced her, then stared into his eyes.

"Eric, making love is an important part of life, even for a pregnant woman. Unless the pregnancy is high risk, there's no reason for anything to change. With time, as the woman gets bigger, modifications are required, but the act itself is perfectly safe. Even three times a night."

"But she was, ah, enjoying herself a lot."

"Lucky her. So she had a few orgasms. Again, this is a part of life. It's natural and safe."

"Yeah?"

"I promise."

He studied her face, searching for hidden truths, but couldn't see anything but love and affection. His fear and panic faded.

"I didn't want to hurt her or the baby."

"I know," CeCe told him. "On behalf of women everywhere, thanks for being one of the good guys. I'm proud of you. Pitifully envious of your sex life, but proud."

Now that he had the answer to his question, he didn't want to be talking about sex with his sister. In fact, he didn't want to be talking to her at all. He'd left Hannah sleeping, and he wanted to get back before she woke up.

He started inching toward the door.

CeCe pinned him with a stared. ''Oh, no you don't. You woke me up, so the least you can do is stay and talk to me.''

''I don't have much to talk about.''

''Sure. Now that you feel better.'' Her gaze turned speculative. ''I'm surprised you're interested in a woman who's pregnant. You've always avoided anything serious. A baby is a lot of reasonability.''

''It's not mine. I'm just dating the mother.''

''What happens when the child is born?''

He hadn't thought that far in advance. Nothing about his relationship with Hannah had followed his normal game plan. He'd never confirmed she was only in it for good times.

''She's only four months pregnant,'' he said.

''Time passes quickly.'' She smiled. ''This could get very interesting.''

Speaking of interest. ''She hasn't told her family she's pregnant. Could you keep the information to yourself?''

CeCe sighed. ''And here I'd planned to spend my morning talking to my co-workers about my brother's sex life. Okay. I won't say anything.''

He hugged her. ''Thanks, sis. You're the best.''

''Cheap talk. Go on. Get out of here.''

He bolted for the door before she could think of any more embarrassing questions to ask.

Eric arrived back at Hannah's place shortly before six. He made his way to her bedroom where he debated joining her or simply waking her to tell her he had to get to work.

If he'd been asked the previous day, he would have said that work always came first and that there was no temptation big enough to keep him from his career goals.

But those intellectual concepts faded in importance when he was faced with a very beautiful, very naked Hannah, curled up asleep. Her blond hair spread across the pillow and curved against one cheek. One bare arm rested outside the covers. He could see the shape of her body under the blanket and sheet, and that, combined with the intimate knowledge he'd gained over the past twelve hours, was more than enough to get him hard.

And once hard, the thought of leaving didn't seem the least bit appealing.

He quickly shed his clothes and slipped into bed beside her. She stirred and rolled toward him, then came awake when she touched his chilled skin.

"Eric?" Her green eyes were sleepy and unfocused. "What's going on?"

"Nothing." He pulled her close.

She started to snuggle close, then stopped, propped herself up on one elbow and stared at him. "You're freezing. What happened?"

"I went out for a while, and I forgot my jacket."

It might be spring, but it was still chilly before dawn. He would guess the temperature had been down in the forties.

She glanced at the clock, then sank down onto the bed. "Went out? This early? Where? Is everything all right?"

"It's fine." He traced the curve of her cheek. "I was worried about you. About what we'd done."

She cuddled close and rested her arm on his chest. "You mean because we made love? That drove you out into the night?"

She sounded both amused and confused.

"Not exactly." He paused. "Okay, yes. I was worried. We were kind of active, and you're pregnant. I wanted to make sure I hadn't hurt the baby."

She looked at him and wrinkled her nose. "At six in the morning? How did you do that?"

"I talked to my sister."

Her eyes widened as her eyebrows lifted. "You did what?"

"I drove over to CeCe's place and talked to her. She says everything is fine and not to worry."

Hannah shrieked and pulled away. As she turned, she pulled the covers over her head.

"What?" he asked, but he could only see a quivering mound. Not a single part of her was visible.

"You talked to your *sister?*" Hannah demanded, her voice slightly muffled.

"I didn't know who else to ask." He put his hand on what he thought was her shoulder. "I didn't want you or the baby to be hurt in any way."

"You told your *sister* we had sex?"

"I had to. Otherwise the question didn't make much sense."

Hannah gave a garbled cry and curled up tighter. "She's going to think I'm a slut," she moaned.

"That's crazy. Why would she think that?"

Hannah threw back the covers and stared at him.

''Oh, I don't know. Maybe because I'm pregnant with another man's child and I'm sleeping with you. It sounds kind of slutty to me.''

He smoothed her hair back from her face. ''Don't say that. You've been very particular about who you've had in bed.''

''How do you know that?''

''Am I wrong?''

She sighed. ''No. Not really. I just...'' She shook her head. ''Did you have to tell your sister?''

''Why does her being a relative make a difference.''

''It just does. She must hate me.''

''Actually, she thought the whole thing was pretty funny.'' He grinned. ''And she was impressed by my stamina.''

Hannah flopped back on her pillow. ''You did *not* say we'd done it three times, did you?''

''Well, I—''

She groaned and pulled the covers back over her head. ''I can never leave this house. Not ever. I'm going to have to stay here until I'm eighty.''

''You're overreacting.''

''Oh, sure. Easy for you to say. You're the guy. In this story all anyone is going to think about you is that you're some kind of a stud. You come off looking great. But me... It's gonna be slut central for sure.''

He chuckled and tugged at the covers. When she didn't release them, he decided on another course of attack.

Eric ducked under the sheet and slid toward her.

When his fingers encountered the smooth skin of her waist, he slipped higher, across her ribs, toward her breasts.

"We are *so* not doing that again," she said, pushing at his hand. "It might be a little late, but I have a reputation to think of. There's nothing you can say to convince me that you'll ever... Ah."

While she'd been busy talking, he'd replaced his fingers with his mouth. Just as she'd promised he couldn't convince her, he'd closed his mouth over her nipple.

Her grip on the blanket loosened as her breath caught. He took advantage of her inattention to push the blankets down to her waist, exposing her to view. Then he licked her nipple and blew on the damp skin.

"This isn't a good idea," she whispered, even as her legs fell open.

"Probably not."

"You have to get to work."

"Agreed. I'll get up in a second."

"Okay."

He slid his hand from her hip to her thigh, then between where he found her already wet. He pushed through the damp curls and found her center.

"How many seconds?" she asked as he began touching her.

He shifted from her breast to her neck. "How many do you need?"

"A couple hundred."

He nibbled his way from her neck to her ear. "It's not going to take you three minutes, is it?"

He shifted so he could keep touching her while

slipping a finger inside. Her muscles were already starting to tighten.

"Maybe just a couple of minutes," she whispered. "Or thirty seconds, or..."

He pulled his hand away and moved between her legs. Slowly, deliberately, he settled his arousal against her and pushed his way inside.

She was tight, slick and hot and despite how many times they'd made love the previous night, he wasn't sure he could hold on for very long. It seemed that no matter how much he had her, he continued to want her. Want to be inside of her.

Maybe it was her responsiveness. The way she arched her head and moaned as she approached her climax. Maybe it was the way her hands fluttered at her sides as he reached between them and rubbed her. Maybe it was the contractions of her release and the way she clung to him, begging him never to stop. Or maybe it was how her body's response pushed him over the edge.

Right now, inside of her, moving back and forth, filling her, feeling her swell around him, he didn't much care. All he knew was that when she reached for his hips, then slid her hands around so she could pull him closer, he simply wanted to explode.

She parted her legs even more, drawing him in. The first of her contractions swept through her and she cried out. Her eyes closed, her mouth parted as she sucked in air. Her entire body shuddered as she lost herself in the pleasure of what they were doing.

He held on as long as he could. He thought of baseball and his staff meeting, but eventually the rubbing and friction took their toll. He felt the building pressure until he had no choice but to give in, plunging deeper and losing himself inside of her.

''You're late,'' Jeanne announced cheerfully as Eric walked into his office. She glanced at the clock. ''Okay, technically it's before eight and your first meeting isn't until nine-thirty, but still. Arriving anytime postsunrise isn't like you.''

Eric grinned at his assistant. After the night—and morning—he'd had, there was nothing she could say to affect his good mood.

''Morning, Jeanne,'' he said as he walked past her.

She stood and followed him.

''That's it?'' she complained. ''You're not going to say anything else? Not even a hint as to what caused you to get in here at a practically normal hour? Was it car trouble? Extra time spent working out? A date that lasted into the wee hours?''

He set his briefcase on his desk, then crossed to the coffeepot. ''Thanks for starting this for me.''

''You're welcome.'' She paused in the doorway. ''I'm waiting.''

His grin broadened. ''I know.''

She sighed. ''Let me guess. You're not going to say a word. You're simply going to let me wonder.''

He poured a mug and took a sip. ''Great coffee.''

''I hate it when you get like this.''

''Sorry.''

''You're not sorry in the least. You're enjoying yourself. It's just so annoying. All of it.'' She huffed out of his office and returned to her desk.

''You could give me a hint,'' she called.

He returned to his desk without responding. As

much as he liked Jeanne, he wasn't going to tell her what she wanted to know. He suspected she already had a good idea about what could have kept him from showing up at his usual time, but there was no need to discuss it. He rarely shared the details of his personal life with anyone.

He glanced at his schedule for the day and saw he had a meeting with Mari later that morning. Remembering her request to talk to him about her project, he called for Jeanne.

She walked into his office. "You want to confess all?"

"No. I need all the information we have on the new biomedical research facility. Wasn't there something about it in the paper?"

"I think so. Let me pull the files and I'll check online for any articles."

"Thanks. I want to be prepared."

Mari Bingham arrived promptly at eleven. Jeanne brought her into his office, and Eric motioned her toward the sofa.

"Let's be comfortable," he said.

"Sure. Thanks for seeing me."

"Not a problem. If you think I can help in some way, I want to be supportive of your project." He settled on the opposite end of the sofa and pointed to the papers spread out on the glass-topped table between them. "I've been doing my reading."

"I see that." Mari picked up a printout of a newspaper article protesting the new research facility. "I've heard that there is no 'bad' publicity, but in this case I have to disagree."

"Their slant seems to be more inflammatory than factual," he said.

"Maybe, but do you think the average reader cares about that?" She tossed the article back on the table. "I'm determined to get the research facility up and running. Medical science is on the brink of so many amazing discoveries in fields of fertility and reproduction. There are diseases that could be cured, even prevented. But so much promising work goes underfunded and overlooked. I think we can change that."

"By bringing cutting-edge scientists together," he said.

She smiled. "You've been reading my reports."

"Sure. You make a good case." He shrugged. "But what you do is out of my realm of expertise. I have nothing to do with funding."

"You're someone upper management listens to." She slid forward on her seat and stared at him. Her hazel eyes were intense, her posture stiff.

Eric looked for similarities between Mari and Hannah—they were cousins—but except for their height and build, he couldn't find any.

"I happen to know there are going to be several meetings on this subject that you'll be attending. I would like you to speak up for the research facility."

"Certainly. As I said, I'm impressed with what you want to do. But with all the controversy, you could have an uphill battle."

Her mouth twisted. "Tell me about it. I'm thinking of bringing in a big gun. A friend of mine from New York. She's experienced in public relations and fundraising."

Eric glanced at the papers in front of him. "I would

suggest you talk to her about coming onboard. Someone outside of the loop can give a fresh perspective. Also, she would have different contacts for the fund-raising. More money is always better, right?''

Mari smiled and relaxed a little. ''Of course. Great idea. I'll call Lillith this afternoon and see if she's available. I've been threatening to drag her out here forever and now I finally have a reason.''

They discussed the upcoming meetings and how Eric could assist her cause. Forty-five minutes later she rose to leave.

''I feel better,'' she said. ''Thank you.''

''My pleasure.''

''No. You didn't have to do this for me, and I want you to know I appreciate the support. If I can ever return the favor, let me know.''

''I will.''

He escorted her to the door.

Later that afternoon Jeanne buzzed him with the announcement that ''A Lisa Paulson is on the phone.''

Eric picked up the receiver. ''Yes?''

''Hi, Eric. I'm from an executive-recruiting firm in Dallas. We've been retained by Bingham Enterprises to fill a position for a junior vice president position. Your name appears on a list of potential candidates. I was wondering if you'd have time to speak with me about that.''

Chapter Twelve

After treating herself to a trim and a manicure, Hannah returned from the Cut 'N' Curl shortly after two. She still felt floaty and otherworldly from the night she'd spent with Eric. If she could bottle the feeling, she could use it to cure about forty percent of the world's ills.

So much had happened in such a short period of time—seeing the ultrasound of the baby, finding out that Eric wanted her but was afraid to act on his desire, then spending the night in his arms.

Last night—and this morning—had been amazing. Not just the physical pleasure, although that had been pretty darned extraordinary, but the rest of it, too. The way they'd talked about everything. Her sense of being safe around him. Lying awake and listening to him breathing, while entertaining the possibility that she could really see herself with him for always.

She pulled into her driveway and climbed out of the car. After walking around the house, Hannah went into the backyard and sat on the grass. She could see the hills in the distance and the tops of the trees ringing the lake below. The sun warmed her arms and back. Her heart beat quickly.

Did she mean that? *Was* she falling for Eric? Falling in love with him?

She thought about her relationship with Matt. While she'd been attracted to him, their time together had been more about him seducing her, emotionally and physically. Everything had happened so fast she'd never had a chance to stop and think about what was going on. So she didn't want to make the same mistake with Eric.

Not that they were even close to being the same man. She'd known Eric forever. She understood what he wanted, what was important to him. He was nothing like Matt. To Eric, truth and honor mattered.

She smiled. He was a good man. The kind of man who cared about her baby even though it wasn't his. The kind of man who would respect her and her dreams.

She flopped back on the grass and stared up at the sky. For a while she'd worried that coming home was too much like running away, but now she was back, it seemed that instead of running *away* from her past she'd been moving *toward* her future. At last she was getting it right.

By six Hannah had put the finishing touches on the romantic dinner she'd prepared. She'd set the small table in the kitchen with her best dishes. A pale-pink linen tablecloth set off the fresh flowers she'd bought at the market.

She'd made a salad and beef Stroganoff. The thick, fragrant entrée simmered on a back burner. As soon as Eric arrived and they were ready to eat, she would stir in the sour cream and serve everything.

She'd changed her clothes, replacing her more casual outfit with a sleeveless dress that buttoned down the front.

"Quite the invitation," she murmured as she stared at herself in the mirror. "Think he'll accept it?"

The thought of Eric slowly, deliberately unfastening her dress, then pushing it aside made her stomach tighten in anticipation. Exactly how long could that main course simmer?

The question made her smile, but what caused her heart to stumble was the sound of a car in her driveway. Hannah hurried to the front door and pulled it open just as Eric climbed the front stairs.

He was so tall and handsome in his suit. His dark eyes flashed with welcome and his broad smile nearly made her float with happiness.

He looked as thrilled as she felt; as delighted as she that they were finally together. There were so many questions she wanted to ask. Had the day dragged for him, as well? Had he watched the clock and counted the hours? Did he want to stay with her through the night and did it seem like the weekend would never get here?

"Hi," she said as he walked into the house.

"Hi, yourself." He shrugged out of his jacket and slung it over the small bench she'd placed by the front door. "Guess what happened today?"

You realized you were in love with me.

The thought stunned her and she was grateful she'd only thought it instead of speaking it out loud. But once planted, the seed of Eric loving her grew until it filled her. That's what she wanted. His love.

"You got a raise," she said instead, because it was safer and she wasn't sure how he would react to what she'd actually been thinking.

"Better," he told her, closing the front door and taking her hand. He led her into the living room. "A recruiter from Dallas called me today about a vice president's position. Isn't that great?"

He waited until she was seated before settling next to her, but didn't seem to notice that she'd collapsed onto the sofa instead of sitting delicately.

"I don't understand," she murmured in shock. "I thought you liked your job."

"I do. I'm learning a lot and contributing to the organization. But the quickest path to promotion is often to be recruited away. Lisa—the recruiter—said she'd heard about me through a couple of different people I've worked with." He paused and frowned slightly. "The director of finance left last year. I'd worked with him quite a bit. I wonder if he gave Lisa my name." He shrugged. "It doesn't matter where she got it, the point is she's impressed and wants to set up a meeting. Oh, and I have to send her a new résumé. I'll need to update the one I have on my computer."

Hannah felt as if the world had fallen off its axis and was spinning out of control. "You're going to meet with her?"

"Sure. It's the first step. Then if I pass muster with

her and the Human Resources Department, I meet with the company's senior executives.'' He stared off into the distance. ''I always thought I'd have to leave town to get a position as vice president, but this one is at Bingham Enterprises. So I wouldn't have to move.''

''That's wonderful,'' she said faintly.

This wasn't happening. It couldn't be. Not after last night. Not after she realized she cared about him.

He continued to explain everything Lisa had told him about the process and what was expected.

''At least I won't have to travel for the interviews,'' he said. ''That will make scheduling easier. Of course, there's so much to do between now and then. I have to research the company and the market. Explore the competition. Maybe come up with some ideas about growing the market.''

He was in the room and talking, but Hannah got the feeling he wasn't actually *with* her anymore. He'd retreated into his own world. One she couldn't be a part of or reach. She wasn't sure if she should shake some sense into him or throw up her hands in defeat.

She decided on the middle ground. ''You sound very excited,'' she said.

''It's an amazing opportunity.''

''It certainly is, and you're smart enough to dazzle them. You're also smart enough to realize that you're having dinner with a beautiful woman who took a lot of time to get ready for her evening with you. You probably want to comment on that. Oh, and mention how great last night was and that you couldn't stop thinking about it. At least until the recruiter called.''

Eric stared at her for a couple of seconds, then smiled sheepishly. "Sorry. I got carried away."

"Just a little."

He leaned toward her and pulled her close. She went into his embrace, and as soon as his arms closed around her, her world righted itself.

"Better?" he asked.

"We're getting there."

He brushed his mouth against hers. "You *are* beautiful. Did you really go to a lot of trouble for me?"

"Absolutely."

"Then I can't wait to check it all out." He touched her cheek. "And you're right. I *couldn't* stop thinking about you or last night, even after the recruiter called."

"I'm glad."

He settled back on the sofa and drew her against him so her head rested on his shoulder.

"Tell me about your day," he said.

Hannah filled him in on the few things she'd done, trying to make it all sound more exciting than it had been.

"Nothing as thrilling as your phone call," she admitted, and let herself think about the opportunity. "The job would be a lot more responsibility."

"I know, but I'm up for the challenge. The truth is I never thought I'd make V.P. before I turned thirty. This really puts me on the fast track."

And still in town, at least for now.

The thought of him leaving the area made her insides all twist up. "Would you really have moved away for the chance at a promotion?"

He stroked her hair. "Executives are expected to

be mobile,'' he said. ''I like it here, but outside of the hospital and Bingham Enterprises, there aren't a lot of opportunities in the area.''

So if the company had been in Texas or California or somewhere else, he would have gone.

Hannah felt lost and confused. A part of her knew the relationship was too new for her to expect anything else from Eric, yet she found herself wanting to say something along the lines of ''How could you leave me?'' Because leave he would. He'd made that clear.

''I'm guessing when they give you the fancy title, they expect a lot in return,'' she said quietly.

''Sure. Long hours, too. To be a junior vice president now—'' he raised one hand palm up and let it fall back on the sofa ''—I'd really have to prove myself.''

But he sounded more thrilled by the prospect than daunted.

''You already work fifty- to sixty-hour weeks. Would you put in more than that?''

He considered the question. ''Probably.''

Her heart clenched. ''So you wouldn't have much time for a social life.''

He smiled at her. ''You sound like my sister. She worries about me working too much.''

''With good reason.'' She shifted so she faced him and decided to pursue the sister angle. Talking about Cecilia was a whole lot safer than talking about herself. ''What do you say when she lectures you?''

''That she needs to get a life.'' He leaned forward and rested his forearms on his thighs. ''Seriously, I know she has a point. That I can't spend my whole life working. Eventually there's the whole family thing. But I don't know. It's not really me."

She wouldn't have been more shocked if he'd slapped her. The family thing wasn't him? Then what was he doing with her? She was a pregnant woman. There was about to be a child in her life and he didn't do the family thing?

She wanted to lash out at him. She wanted to scream her protests and tell him he'd been wrong to lead her on and let her believe they could have something. Because she was all about family. All she wanted was someone to love who would love her back. She wanted to be first in someone's world.

She'd thought that someone could be Eric. Being wrong had never hurt so much.

Her eyes burned, her arms and legs felt heavy, and it was all she could do not to give in to tears. But she didn't. Because she and Eric had never discussed the future. They'd never talked about what each of them wanted, although maybe they should have before last night. She'd thought he wanted what she wanted. Especially after he found out she was pregnant and had been okay with it. Now she knew that he hadn't minded because he'd never expected there to be anything significant between them.

She had to get him out of here before she broke down completely.

"Look," she said, forcing herself to smile. "You've got a thousand things on your mind and a résumé to update. We can do dinner another time."

His expression of eagerness stabbed at her.

"You sure you don't mind?" he asked. "I know you went to a lot of trouble for dinner."

"It'll freeze. We'll take a rain check on this. It's fine. Really."

More than fine. She needed him gone so she could lick her wounds. She wanted to crawl into bed and never get out again.

"You're the best," Eric said. He kissed her cheek, then stood. "I'll give you a call tomorrow."

"Sure. That would be great."

The words sounded good, she thought, wondering when she'd become such an accomplished liar. She didn't think Eric would call, and she was going to do her best not to be happy if he did. Eric wasn't for her. She had to figure out a way to really believe that, and adjust her dreams accordingly.

Lisa Paulson was a tall woman in her forties. While the Bingham Enterprises Human Resources director was at the interview, Lisa was obviously in charge and she wanted to make sure everyone knew. Between his sister and his assistant, Eric was more than used to bossy women and he had no problem dealing with Lisa's strident personality. As she shifted from topic to topic, he wondered if her difficult style was as much a part of the interview process as the questions. If he didn't get riled with her, he wouldn't get riled by difficult employees.

"What is one of your flaws?" she asked. "And please don't say it's that you work too hard. That answer is really boring."

Eric smiled. "I do work too hard, but I don't think of it as a flaw." He considered the question. "I have high expectations for the people who work for me. At times I've been told they're too high. To mitigate that,

I work with my team so we can define our goals together and create a plan to meet them.''

Lisa stared at him for several seconds then made a note on her pad. ''All right, Eric. Give me a minute.'' She rose and left the room.

Eric turned to the Human Resources director—a balding man in his thirties—and asked, ''Did you have any questions for me?''

The man grinned. ''I'm just here to listen. Lisa's tough, but she has a way of cutting to the heart of the matter. We've found some great candidates through her. For what it's worth, you did very well.''

''Thank you.''

Eric tried not to show his surprise. Usually the interviewers didn't give feedback.

When the door to the conference room opened, Lisa returned, followed by Geoff Bingham. As the eldest son, he was the heir apparent to the company.

''Hello, Eric,'' he said.

Eric stood and shook hands. ''Geoff. Good to see you.''

''I wanted Geoff to meet you,'' Lisa said. ''I didn't realize you two were acquainted.''

''It's a small-town thing,'' Eric said with a smile. ''We all know each other.''

Lisa raised her eyebrows. ''So I don't need to tell you about Eric.''

''Probably not,'' Geoff said cheerfully. ''But you will.''

''You're right. You'll get my report before I leave.'' She turned to Eric. ''It was nice to meet you.''

She left, along with the man from Human Resources. Geoff motioned to a seat and took one for himself.

"Lisa is impressed," Geoff said. "That doesn't happen often."

"Thanks. She's a tough interviewer."

"I know. That's why we hired her." He leaned back in his chair. "She found you on her own, but when she presented her list of candidates to me, I was ready to add your name myself."

Another surprise, Eric thought. While he and Geoff had been acquaintances for years, they'd never worked together.

"May I ask why?"

Geoff nodded. "Sure. Mari mentioned you a couple of days ago. Between you and me, she couldn't say enough. What impressed her the most was that you'd go out of your way to help her, when there was nothing in it for you."

"I think her research facility will be an asset to the hospital and the community. That's why I supported it."

Geoff nodded. "You'd be surprised how many people aren't willing to do the right thing without there being a motivation of personal gain. You impressed her, and when she told me what happened, I knew I wanted you on the slate for this job. You're the sort of person we want here at Bingham."

"Thank you."

Geoff rose and offered his hand. "Someone will be in touch shortly, Eric. You've made the cut for the next round."

"Great."

They shook hands again, and Eric headed for the front entrance of the main building.

He did his best to keep from grinning like a fool, but what he wanted to do was yell out his success. Hot damn! Most of the time there was a waiting period after an interview, but not today.

There was going to be stiff competition with the next round, but he wasn't worried. He'd work through the night if necessary to get his presentation just right.

As he walked to his car, he made a mental list of everything he had to do. Call and thank Mari for one. And get in touch with Hannah. She'd been so understanding the other night. He should send her flowers. And maybe drop by to see her.

He glanced at his watch and saw it was barely two in the afternoon. Would she be home now and open to a little company? He found himself wanting to tell her what had happened during the interview. He wanted to celebrate with her in all the best ways possible. Including both of them getting naked. He couldn't remember the last time he'd wanted to take the afternoon off work…then he grinned.

Sure he could. And that time had been about Hannah, too. There was something about that woman. Something that made him want to be with her all the time.

He got in his car and headed for the hospital. He would check in with Jeanne, then give Hannah a call and see if she was available. If so, he would duck out and go to her place. He knew she would be as excited about his interview as he was.

When he arrived at his office, he found Jeanne pacing in the waiting area. The second she saw him, she rushed forward. Worry darkened her eyes and drew her eyebrows together.

"I thought you'd never get back," she said. "Oh, Eric."

He grabbed her arm, but before he could ask what was wrong, she started speaking again.

"It's Hannah. She's in trouble. There's something wrong. You have to go to the clinic right away."

Eric didn't remember leaving his office or racing across the glassed-in walkway between the hospital and the clinic. When he burst into the waiting room, he ran to the reception window and announced himself.

"I'm here to see Hannah Bingham. There's something wrong and she needs me."

The young woman nodded. "Yes, Mr. Mendoza. I've been told to expect you. Right this way."

She led him into a small room with a window. Hannah lay on a hospital bed. An IV dripped fluid into her arm. She was pale, damp with sweat and lying so still, his heart stopped.

"Hannah," he breathed. Behind him he heard the receptionist leave.

Hannah's eyes opened. The irises were startlingly green against her pale skin. Her lips moved, but she didn't speak. Then a single tear spilled from the corner of her eye and dripped into her hair.

He sprinted to her side and took her hand in his. "Tell me," he whispered, brushing her hair from her face. "Tell me what's going on."

"I h-have to stay calm," she murmured. "For the baby."

The relief was sweet. She hadn't lost the baby. He bent over her and kissed her forehead. ''Keep breathing,'' he told her. ''I'm right here.''

Just then the door opened and a woman in white coat entered. She introduced herself as Dr. Rhonda Severs.

''You're going to be fine,'' she told Hannah, then looked at him. ''Hannah's been feeling poorly for the past couple of days. She got dizzy and came in this morning. It seems she picked up a virus somewhere. Nothing to hurt the baby,'' she added quickly. ''Unfortunately, the virus is causing her blood pressure to spike.''

For the first time, Eric noticed the automatic blood pressure cuff around Hannah's left arm.

''You've been sick for two days,'' he said, turning back to Hannah. He'd just seen her three nights ago. ''Why didn't you call me?''

''You were busy getting ready for your interview. I didn't want to be a bother.''

''She's going to have to be one now,'' Dr. Severs said cheerfully. ''Hannah is going to have to fight this virus with plenty of rest. She's to stay off her feet for about a week.''

Hannah clutched his arm. ''I didn't know who else to call. I just need you to take me home. I'll get someone else in to take care of things.'' Another tear escaped. ''I can't lose the baby.''

''You won't,'' her doctor promised. ''I know you're scared, and that's understandable. But you're going to be fine.''

''Of course she is,'' Eric said with a confidence he didn't feel. Hannah's terror was a tangible creature in the room. He was scared for her, and determined to do what he could to get her through this.

''I'll take care of everything,'' he said to the doctor. ''Just give me a list of instructions.''

''Eric,'' Hannah whispered. ''You can't.''

''Sure I can. I have plenty of vacation time built up. I'll move in and take over your life.'' He smiled at her. ''You'll love it.''

Her lips pressed together. ''Really? You'd do that for me?''

''Of course. Now you stop worrying about everything except getting better. Leave the rest of it to me.''

He turned back to the doctor and listened while she gave him instructions. Except for Hannah staying off her feet and staying hydrated, the rest of it was common sense. Dr. Severs promised to send a nurse in to show him how to use the blood pressure cuff they would be taking home with them.

For the first time since that morning, when she'd gotten so dizzy that she'd nearly passed out, Hannah allowed herself to let go of a little of the fear. Knowing that she wasn't going to be alone eased a large portion of her worries. Between Eric's willingness to help out and her doctor's promise that she and the baby would be fine, Hannah found herself breathing a little easier.

The guilt was still there, though. She'd been feeling sick for nearly three days, but she'd assumed the upset stomach and pounding headache were from missing Eric rather than from a virus of some kind. If she'd thought otherwise, she might have come into the clinic sooner.

She watched him with the doctor. Was he really going to help her? She'd figured once she got home she would have to call her grandmother, or a home care service of some kind. She'd never thought Eric would bother. After all, he'd said family wasn't his thing.

But maybe she'd been too quick to judge him. Maybe he'd spoken without thinking that something in his life was different. Namely her and the baby. When he'd burst into the room just now, he'd looked as scared as she'd felt. That had to mean something.

The possibility that it wasn't over made her cry even more. She'd missed him so much. More than she should have. More than was wise. She'd been so busy wondering what he felt about her that she'd never stopped to think about what she felt. It had taken him leaving for her to realize she was well on her way to falling for him.

Dr. Severs squeezed her hand. "See you in a couple of days. If you have any questions, please call. You have my beeper number, right?"

Hannah nodded. When they were alone, Eric turned to her.

"Let's go home," he said.

She smiled through her tears, knowing they were the best words he could have said.

Chapter Thirteen

They arrived back at her house in Eric's car. Hannah lay on the back seat and tried to relax, but it was difficult with so much fear pulsing through her body. She knew worrying wouldn't help and that she had to take the doctor's words on faith, but all she could think about was the baby. She didn't want anything to happen to her child.

"How are you doing?" Eric asked as he opened the back door.

"Okay."

She sat up and slid to the edge of the seat, but before she could stand to walk inside, he held up a restraining hand.

"Stay here until I get the front door open and we have a clear run at the bedroom."

She nodded and passed over her purse. When he returned, she started to stand.

‘‘Not so fast,’’ he told her as he bent close and gathered her in his arms.

‘‘Eric, no! You’ll hurt yourself.’’

He smiled at her. ‘‘Hey, I’m a tough, macho guy.’’

‘‘Yeah, and I’m seriously pregnant.’’

‘‘You’re barely showing, and I can handle it. Now hang on and enjoy the ride.’’

She gave in to the feeling of being close to him and wrapped her arms around his neck. When they were inside, he carried her to the bedroom and set her on the edge of the mattress.

‘‘What do you want to change into?’’ he asked. ‘‘Nightgown? Sweats and a T-shirt?’’

Hannah considered the question. If she was going to be spending all her time in bed, she wanted to be comfortable, but not worry about flashing the world.

‘‘Sweats would be good.’’ She pointed to her dresser. ‘‘I have some cotton ones with a drawstring waist in that bottom drawer. T-shirts are in the middle drawer.’’

He brought her the clothes, then left her alone to get changed. When she was done, she curled up on the bed and listened to him speak on the phone. He was explaining the situation to Jeanne and having her rearrange his schedule so he could stay with Hannah the next day.

When he walked into the room, she rolled onto her back.

‘‘You don’t have to give up your life for me,’’ she told him, trying to sound firm and in control. ‘‘Work is important to you, and you need to be there.’’

He sat on the edge of the bed and took her hand. ‘‘I’m taking the rest of today off and tomorrow. We’ll play it by ear after that. Don't worry.'' He smoothed the hair off her forehead. ''As I said before, I have plenty of vacation time. Right now, keeping you and the baby healthy are my main priorities. Now, I need to run to my place and get a few things. Will you be all right on your own for about forty-five minutes?''

She nodded and he kissed her cheek. ''I'll be right back.'' He grinned. ''Don't go anywhere.''

She managed a weak smile. ''I won't.''

When he was gone, she curled back on her side and tried not to cry. She was scared and confused but also happy. Happy because Eric wanted to be here for her. She couldn't believe how caring he'd become. Nothing he was doing made sense in light of what he'd said the other night.

Maybe that was it, she told herself. Maybe he'd said what he always believed to be true, while his actions spoke what was in his heart.

Pleased and comforted, she closed her eyes and slowed her breathing. For whatever reason, Eric was going to be with her through this time. She wasn't alone. She could cling to that fact and what the doctor had said. She and the baby were going to be fine.

She touched her stomach. ''I promise,'' she whispered. ''You'll see.''

Eric returned within the hour. He brought a small suitcase, a briefcase full of work and a box with a computer game set up. The latter made her raise her eyebrows.

''Yours?'' she asked teasingly.

''Yeah, yeah. I know. A complete waste of time. Sometimes I play it to unwind. I thought it would be something you could do in here.'' He pointed to the TV against the wall opposite her bed.

''I've never been much of a game person, but this is probably the time to take up the hobby. Thank you.''

Thoughtful, she told herself. The man was thoughtful.

''Jeanne cleared my schedule for tomorrow,'' he said, sitting on the edge of the bed. ''So we'll see how it goes. If you need me here on Friday, then I'm your guy.''

As much as she would love him to stay with her for the next week, she knew she had to be realistic. ''I'll be okay.''

''Let's decide Friday morning, okay? In the meantime, I brought sheets and a couple of pillows. I'll camp out next door.''

Next door was the baby's room. There was a rocking chair and a lamp, but little else.

''I don't have any furniture in there,'' she said.

''Even if you did, I wouldn't exactly fit in the crib.'' He shrugged. ''I'll crash on the floor.''

''Why?'' She glanced at the vast expanse of the king-size bed. ''There's plenty of room.''

''I know, but...''

His reticence made no sense. It wasn't as if they hadn't slept together before.

''Do I snore?'' she asked.

''No.'' He chuckled. ''Okay, here's the thing. I'm not sure I can share a bed with you now. Not without...''

He turned away, but not before she caught the change in his expression. Was Eric embarrassed?

"What?" she asked. "Tell me, please. Is it the baby? Are you afraid you'd hurt me?"

He looked back at her. "Yes, but not in the way you mean." He cupped her chin and rubbed his thumb across her mouth. "I want you, Hannah. Sharing a bed will be uncomfortable."

His words delighted her. Despite everything, he still thought she was sexy enough to be a temptation. Right this second she felt about as appealing as a dishrag, but that was okay. Eric saw beyond the tears, the growing belly and her fears.

"We can't, well, you know. Not until my blood pressure returns to normal," she said. "But there are other things to do."

He feigned shock. "Were would a nice girl like you learn about that sort of thing?"

"Extension courses."

He laughed. The deep, throaty sound filled her with happiness.

"Not necessary," he told her. "But if you're offering a piece of the bed, I'll take it over the floor. And I'll do my best to keep my animal urges to myself."

"Just until I'm better," she said.

"Absolutely."

"You did great," Hannah said.

Eric cleared the plate from her lap table. "You think?"

She smiled. "I'm impressed. Really. I didn't know you could cook."

He chuckled. "Neither did I. I had to call CeCe twice to make sure I had everything right." He picked up his plate from the nightstand. "Does it really matter if I use oregano rather than basil?"

"Ah, yes. Spices make a big difference. You're going to have to trust me on that."

He nodded toward the door. "I'll take these to the kitchen and clean up the mess I made while cooking."

She wrinkled her nose. "I feel guilty that you have to do all of that."

"Don't sweat it. Plunging my hands in hot soapy water is probably character building or something. I'll survive it."

"Okay. Thanks."

He left with the plates. As he walked through the living room he decided it was a good thing Hannah couldn't get up right now. If she saw the state of her kitchen, she would pass out. Or kill him.

He stared at the pots and pans littering the counter, the open yet empty cans of ingredients, the bottles of spices, the boiled-over mess on the stove. He had his work cut out for him. But first he had a call to make.

He picked up the phone and dialed his sister's number. She answered on the first ring.

"Did you burn it?"

"No. Dinner was great."

CeCe laughed. "You're lying."

"I'm not. The chicken was cooked but not tough, the vegetables were a little soft, but that's okay. The rice was difficult. I thought you just boiled it until it was done."

"Not exactly." She sighed. "Where did I go wrong with you, little brother?"

"You didn't. I'm perfect."

"Uh-huh. Sure you are. And now you have to clean up everything."

"I was just thinking that myself. I don't suppose you want to come over and help?"

"Not even on a bet. Let me know if you need menus and recipes for tomorrow."

"I was thinking we'd do take-out," he said.

"So you're staying there?" CeCe sounded both surprised and curious.

"I think so. Hannah needs someone, and I don't mind being here."

"Interesting."

He didn't like the sound of that. "We're friends," he insisted.

"Friends who sleep together."

He wasn't about to discuss that with CeCe. "Irrelevant."

"I think it's extremely relevant. You've never taken responsibility for anyone before. I'm not saying that's bad," she added quickly. "I'm saying your goals have been about your career, not other people."

"Hannah isn't a goal. She's..."

He wanted to say "someone he cared about" but his sister would run with that one.

"I don't want anything to happen to her or the baby," he said instead.

"I know, and I'm glad you feel that way. I just think the whole situation is fascinating. Keep me posted."

"Yeah, right. I'll be calling to dish at least three times a day."

She chuckled. "I wouldn't have thought you even knew what dishing was." She sighed. "Seriously,

Eric, call me if anything happens. I mean it. I want Hannah and her baby to be okay, too."

"Thanks, sis. I will."

He hung up and leaned against the counter.

He understood the point his sister had been trying to make. That in the past, he'd chosen women who didn't need or expect taking care of. He'd only ever been responsible for himself. Even when his mother had been sick and dying, CeCe had shouldered the burden herself, keeping the worst of the news and the prognosis from him until nearly the end.

He'd never thought to be angry with her for it. He'd understood she'd been doing her best to let him focus on building his career and finishing grad school. She'd known about his dreams of success, and she'd wanted that for him. Maybe she'd also done it out of guilt.

Eric had never been close with his mother. CeCe had told stories of a bright, happy woman who baked and offered hugs and told stories. Maybe she'd been like that when CeCe had been young, but he'd never met that woman. His mother had been withdrawn and distant. As he'd grown up, he'd learned that his father had charmed her, then left her pregnant and destitute after stealing her life savings, along with the money from the insurance after the death of CeCe's father. Eric had learned he wasn't just a bastard by birth, but also that he'd been born to one.

Over the years he'd pieced together different stories about his father. The man had been handsome, charming and the kind of person who spent his life using people. Not exactly a heritage to make one proud. Eric had vowed to be different. To make sure he never used anyone. And the easiest way he knew to do that was never to get seriously involved.

He glanced toward the living room and the bedroom beyond. So where did that philosophy leave him now? Was he involved? He shrugged. How could he not be? He was living with Hannah, taking care of her. He supposed there was an inherent risk, but he couldn't walk away. Not now. He wanted her and the baby to be safe. He *needed* to make sure they both pulled through this. And the hell of it was, he couldn't say why.

He was willing to admit Hannah wasn't like the other women he'd dated. They'd never had the conversation about a commitment-free relationship, and he'd realized there was no point in having it now. Mostly because he already knew the answer to the question. Hannah didn't do simple and easy. She was looking for a whole lot more. Which meant he didn't belong here.

Only it was too late to back out now. He had to stay, at least through this crisis. And then what? Did he duck out while the getting was still good or did he ride this train to the end of the line?

What would he find when he got there? Happiness? A future? He shook his head. In his world love never lasted, and happily ever after was something people only ever saw in the movies.

''Knock, knock,'' a voice called.

Hannah put down her book and smiled. ''In here, Jeanne. The bedroom's in the back.''

''Ooh, I love what you've done with the living room. Is the sofa new?'' Jeanne walked into the bedroom with a large take-out bag in one hand and two bottles of water in the other. ''Did you get that sofa in town or was it a special order? It's beautiful. Great color choices.''

''Thanks. It was a special order, but from a local store. Millers'.''

Jeanne set one bottle of water on Hannah's lap table and the other on the nightstand. ''How did you get it so quickly?''

Hannah grinned. ''It was a reject. Apparently whoever ordered it hated it on sight. So the sofa was in the store as a consignment sale. I loved it immediately, which I have to tell you made me question my taste.''

Jeanne shook her head. ''I'm with you. It's terrific. I may have to go check out patterns and styles this weekend.'' She plopped down in the chair and looked at Hannah. ''So, how are you?''

''Desperately bored and grateful for your company. Thanks for bringing me lunch.''

''Hey, it got me out of the office. I should be thanking you.''

She pulled deli sandwiches out of the bag, along with several small containers of salad. Plastic forks and napkins followed.

''How are you feeling?'' Jeanne asked.

''Good.'' Hannah nodded at the blood pressure cuff next to her on the bed. ''My 11 a.m. reading was completely normal. I don't have a temperature, I'm drinking enough fluids to float the entire Spanish Armada, which means plenty of trips to the bathroom, but as those are my only outings of the day, I actually look forward to them.''

Jeanne passed over a turkey sandwich. ‘‘Kid, I have to tell you, that sounds pathetic.’’

‘‘I know.’’ She pushed her book aside and opened the sandwich wrapper. ‘‘I’m not a daytime TV person, which cuts down on my entertainment.’’

‘‘I love soaps,’’ Jeanne confided. ‘‘All that angst and infighting makes my life look completely normal.’’

‘‘I hadn’t thought of it that way.’’

Jeanne held out a container of potato salad. ‘‘Low salt, even. Who knew such a thing was possible.’’

‘‘Thanks.’’ Hannah opened the container and took a bite. ‘‘Not bad.’’

‘‘You’re *so* lying.’’

Hannah laughed. ‘‘Okay, it needs salt, but until I have normal blood pressure for many days in a row, I have to avoid it.’’

‘‘At least your ankles won’t get puffy.’’

‘‘That’s true.’’

Jeanne took a bite of her sandwich and chewed. When she’d swallowed, she said. ‘‘Eric said to say hi. He’s going to want a full report when I get back.’’

‘‘He’s being very sweet about all of this,’’ Hannah said, trying not to look too dopey as she spoke. Just thinking about Eric made her want to beam or burst into song.

Over the past couple of days, he’d been nothing but amazing. He’d stayed with her, worried about her, hovered, cooked, cleaned and slept with his arm around her. She’d discovered that she liked waking up with him next to her. She liked the feel of his body against hers and the sound of his breathing in the silence of the night. She liked *him.* Maybe more than liked. Maybe much more.

Finally this morning she'd insisted he go to work. Just to catch up.

"I find the entire situation really interesting," Jeanne admitted. "He's the sort of man who has always had women throwing themselves at him. He's only ever had to worry about himself. Now he has you and the baby. That's been a big change, but a good one."

Hannah didn't want to read too much in the situation, or wish for too much. "We're just friends."

Jeanne didn't look convinced. "I think he has it bad."

I hope you're right, she thought to herself. But what she said instead was, "So which soaps would you recommend? I know nothing about any of them. Which have the most normal plot lines?"

Jeanne laughed. "Honey, you don't want normal. You want outrageous. The whole point is to be swept away. Okay, what time is it? Oh! My favorite is just coming on. Where's the remote?"

Saturday afternoon Eric lay on Hannah's bed and scanned the book he held. "There are too many choices," he said as he turned the page. "I didn't know there were this many name possibilities in the world."

"I know." Hannah stretched out next to him, one hand on her stomach, her head on his shoulder as she read along with him. "I'm leaning toward finding out if I'm having a boy or a girl. It would simplify things."

"Cut the decision making in half," he agreed, then glanced at her. "You know you're having a boy."

She pushed at his arm. "Quit saying that. You're going to have to eat crow if you're wrong, you know."

"The crows must hate that saying," he told her as he turned the page. "Besides, I'm always right."

"I'm ignoring that." She turned and looked out the window. "It looks really beautiful outside today," she said wistfully.

"We're going. Just give it another half hour. I want the sun to be on the other side of the house so you're in shade. It's pretty warm out there."

She smiled at him. "You're being really silly," she said. "Sitting in the sun isn't going to hurt me."

"I'm not taking any chances."

She sighed and shifted her hand from her stomach to his chest. "Weird, but very sweet."

"Gee, thanks."

He dropped the book on the bed and leaned back against the pillows. He couldn't remember the last Saturday he'd spent in bed...even with a beautiful woman. Usually he was out doing things—often he was at the office. But not today. Today he was going to hang out with Hannah.

He put his hand on top of hers and laced their fingers together. Her closeness, not to mention the way she ran her bare foot up and down his leg, was having a predictable result, but he was determined not to notice. So what if he wanted her? Making love was out of the question and if being close to her was erotic torture, then he would just have to take it like a man.

"I'll bet my garden's changed," she said snuggling close. "In the spring everything grows so quickly."

"You'll see it soon, and I'm sure you'll point out everything that's different."

"Probably," she said cheerfully. "I hope the weeds haven't taken over. I'll bet they know I can't get to them right now and are making a run at claiming the flower beds."

He looked at her. "You think the weeds have committee meetings and a battle plan?"

"Maybe. It would be just like them."

Her eyes were a vivid green. Cats' eyes, he'd always thought. This close he could see the individual flecks of color and the length of her lashes. Her skin was pale and clear, with just a hint of pink on her cheeks.

She was beautiful, completely feminine and the most sexually appealing woman he'd ever known.

His body responded to the thought by sending blood south. He shifted slightly, cursing his decision to pull on sweats that morning. At least in jeans he would have had a prayer of disguising his condition. Instead he was going to have to think virtuous thoughts and hope the condition went away before Hannah noticed.

"I'll weed your garden," he said. "You can sit in the shade and give me directions. How's that?"

Her mouth parted. "Really? You'd do that for me? But you hate my garden."

"I don't hate it. I don't love it the way you do, but so what? This is important to you, and I'm happy to help."

"Oh, Eric." She wrapped both arms around him

and leaned in close. "You are too good for words. Really." She pressed her mouth to his.

He did his best not to get lost in the brief kiss. Unfortunately he was already half-gone, so the light brush of skin against skin nearly made him groan.

"Now don't get all mushy on me," he said, going for a casual tone of voice and hoping he didn't sound as desperate and hungry as he felt.

She looked at him. "I thought you liked us kissing."

"I do, it's just…" How to explain without sounding like a complete dog.

Then, before he could find the words, she slid one hand down his belly and settled it on his erection.

He groaned. "I was hoping you wouldn't notice."

"Why? I like that you want me."

Good to know. "It doesn't mean anything," he said, motioning to his crotch. "It'll go away on its own. I just need a distraction."

Hannah figured that was a not-so-subtle hint that she should move her hand, but she didn't want to. She liked the feel of his hardness and the way he flexed when she stroked him.

"I've missed us making love," she admitted in a whisper.

"Me, too. Spending the night with you is terrific. And torture."

His eyes dilated and his breathing quickened as she continued to move her hand.

"Hannah."

"Shh. Just let me touch you."

She slipped her hand under the waistband of his

sweats and boxer shorts so she could touch him, skin to skin.

He felt good. Silky softness over tensile steel. She traced the tip of him with her finger, then took him in her hand and began to move up and down.

"What are you doing?" he asked in a strangled voice.

"I would think that was obvious."

"But you don't have to do this."

She withdrew her hand and reached for his. After parting her thighs, she escorted him under her night-gown to her panties. She pulled the fabric aside and shifted her hips.

"Touch me," she whispered.

He slid against her slick, wet, swollen flesh. It felt delicious and she hated to pull back, but she tugged his hand free.

"I like touching you," she said. "It turns me on."

"But you can't...we shouldn't."

"You're right. I want to wait and talk to the doctor before I do anything, but that doesn't mean *you* have to suffer."

"I'll wait, too."

She smiled. "But I don't want you to."

She tugged at his sweats until his arousal sprang free. He was hard and masculine and she couldn't wait to touch him again.

She reached for him and began to stroke him. Eric finally gave in and lay back on the bed. He wrapped one arm around her, pulling her close. She lay half on top of him, kissing him while she continued to touch him.

She matched her movements to his breathing. As

he tensed and got closer, she moved faster. When his body stiffened, she raised her head and watched him reach his climax. At the pinnacle of his pleasure, he opened his eyes and stared at her.

She felt as if she could see down to his soul. At that moment, they connected. Hannah felt it and was changed by it.

If there had been doubts before, she now knew the truth. She'd fallen in love with him.

Chapter Fourteen

Monday Jeanne brought lunch again. After a fun-filled hour of laughter and joking, Jeanne headed back to work. Hannah picked up her book and prepared to read away the time until Eric got home from work when she heard a knocking at the front door. Before she could decide if she would be heard yelling for the person to announce themselves, the door opened.

"Hannah? It's your grandmother. May I come in?"

Hannah felt her jaw drop. She glanced around frantically, looking for a place to hide, even as she heard footsteps in the entryway.

"Hannah?" Myrtle called again.

"In here," Hannah answered, wondering what on earth her grandmother was doing here and how she was going to explain lying in bed in the middle of the afternoon.

"How are you, dear?" her grandmother asked as she walked into the bedroom.

As always Myrtle Bingham was perfectly dressed for the occasion. In this case, visiting someone at home. She wore a tailored pantsuit that hinted at a still-trim figure, understated gold jewelry and a handbag that matched her beige shoes.

Hannah felt like a street urchin in her ratty shorts and T-shirt. Her feet were bare and she was in desperate need of a pedicure. At least she'd showered that morning, so she was clean and her hair looked halfway decent.

"I'm, ah, good," Hannah said, then bit her lower lip. "This is a surprise. You dropping by. Not that you're not always welcome. It's just..."

Myrtle motioned to the chair by the bed. When Hannah nodded, the older woman seated herself.

"I attended one of my committee meetings this morning. As we concern ourselves with fund-raising for the clinic, several of the staff there also attend. They are so good about letting us know their needs."

Hannah listened intently, but her mind had already jumped ahead to the punch line. She had a bad feeling that someone at the meeting had spilled the baby news, so to speak. Seconds later she found out she was right.

"One of the nurses spoke to me privately," Myrtle continued. "She said she knew I must be concerned about you and the baby, but that I shouldn't worry too much. You were doing well on your bed rest and everyone expected you to be cleared for regular activities at your doctor's appointment tomorrow."

Myrtle paused expectantly. ‘‘I’m sure there’s a perfectly logical explanation for what she said.’’

Hannah nodded slowly. ‘‘There is. Of course. It’s what you think. I’m pregnant.’’

‘‘I see.’’ Her grandmother’s sharp gaze never left her face. ‘‘I have so many questions, I’m not sure where to start.’’

Hardly a surprise. ‘‘You want to know how far along I am and who the father is and that sort of thing.’’

Her grandmother frowned slightly. ‘‘Yes, I suppose that’s important, too. But what most concerns me is why you didn’t come tell me yourself.’’ Her mouth pulled into a straight line. ‘‘I thought you considered us your family, Hannah. I *am* your grandmother. If you’re in trouble—’’

‘‘I’m not,’’ Hannah said quickly, then had to laugh. ‘‘Well, except for the obvious. Being pregnant, I mean.’’

She looked at the woman sitting next to her. ‘‘I thought you’d be disappointed,’’ she whispered, suddenly fighting tears. ‘‘You weren’t happy that I’d left law school, and I thought hearing about my pregnancy would be too much. I knew you’d find out eventually. It’s not exactly something I can hide.’’

‘‘I was sorry you left Yale,’’ her grandmother admitted, ‘‘but only because I didn’t understand why. Learning about the baby explained so much. Why you left. Why you came back here. Why you bought the house. As for being disappointed, it has never crossed my mind.’’

Hannah wished she could believe her. ‘‘There’s

some element of history repeating itself,'' she said. ''First my mother, now me.''

Myrtle shook her head. ''I don't blame your mother for what happened. That was entirely my son. Billy was wild, and very much a lady's man. He preyed on innocent young women and took advantage of them.''

''So this *is* history repeating itself,'' Hannah said, more than a little embarrassed by the realization.

''No, dear. I just explained it wasn't her fault.''

Hannah shifted so she could sit cross-legged. ''Maybe it wasn't mine, either. I have a bad feeling I fell for the same line my mom did.''

She briefly explained about Matt.

''I see,'' her grandmother said when she'd finished. ''Are you sure you want this young man out of the picture? Shouldn't he be forced to live up to his responsibilities?''

Now Myrtle sounded like Eric, Hannah thought, trying not to smile. ''I understand your point, but I would rather he simply disappeared. I think my child will be much happier with a stable life rather than always hoping his or her father will show up and then being constantly disappointed.''

''I see your point. By the time Billy found out about you, he'd matured to the point where he could consider being a father. But when you were first born, his involvement would have been a disaster.''

The older woman leaned forward. ''Hannah, I wish you felt that you belonged in the family. We all care about you.''

''Thank you.'' Hannah thought about her encounters with her uncle Ron and knew he was on her side. ''I don't blame you or the family. I think I've been reluctant to get too involved. I'm not sure why. Maybe fear of being rejected.''

Myrtle slid the chair closer and took Hannah's hand. ''Never that, dear. I want us to be close. Things may be a little awkward at first as we get to know each other, but I think we can weather the storm. Besides, you're carrying my first great-grandchild.''

''That's true.''

She hadn't considered that her baby would have a connection with the Bingham family, and suddenly she wanted her child to be a part of that heritage. Her baby would know where he or she had come from.

''I'm sorry,'' Hannah said. ''For being standoffish and solitary. I want us to be closer, too.''

''Good.'' Her grandmother squeezed her fingers, then released them. ''How much longer do you have to stay in bed?''

''I see the doctor tomorrow. I'm pretty sure the virus is gone, and my blood pressure has been normal for several days, so I expect I'll be able to return to my regular activities.''

''That's wonderful news! Would you like to move into the family house with me?''

Hannah had been expecting an invitation to lunch, not her own house key. ''If it's all right with you, I'd rather stay here. I have a garden to take care of and a nursery to get ready.'' She held up her hand before her grandmother could say anything. ''I'll check all this with the doctor first, I promise.''

''If you're sure. You'd be more than welcome, Hannah. And the house is big enough for you to have your own space, as you young people like to say.''

Hannah didn't think ''young people'' had been

talking about their own space for nearly twenty years, but she understood what her grandmother was saying. While she appreciated the invitation, she really did want to stay independent. Not to be difficult, but because it was important to her. There was also Eric to consider. Their growing relationship might not flourish under the watchful eye of the Bingham clan.

"If I change my mind, I'll be sure to let you know," Hannah said. "In the meantime, please consider yourself welcome here anytime."

"As you are, dear," her grandmother said. "I want you to promise to take care of yourself. You have a future generation to think of." Her gaze turned speculative. "We're also going to have to think about getting you married."

Hannah laughed. "One thing at a time. Right now I just want permission to walk to the kitchen and back."

"Yes. Of course."

Besides, Hannah thought happily. She might already have the love and marriage thing covered.

Hannah practically bounced out of the doctor's office.

"Isn't this the best news?" she said to Eric as they walked into the main hallway. "I can get up and move around. I can even garden."

"You have to spend an hour in the morning and two hours in the afternoon resting," he reminded her. "And take your blood pressure a couple of times a day."

"Easy to do," she said.

After an entire week in bed, she found the thought

of walking to the kitchen for a pot of tea, or sitting outside, thrilling beyond words. She had, in fact, been cleared for *all* physical activities. When Eric had stepped out of the room to give her privacy to change her clothes, Hannah had made sure to ask the doctor about making love. She'd received a firm thumbs-up.

In fact she had big plans for that afternoon.

She followed Eric to his car, then slid into the passenger's seat.

"You look happy," he said as he settled in next to her and started the engine.

"I am. It's like getting out of prison."

"Oh? How would you know what that feels like?"

She laughed. "Okay, so I don't *know* exactly. But I can imagine. Being confined to bed was pure torture." She touched her stomach. "Although I'd do it all again if necessary."

"I don't think you're going to have to," he said. "Dr. Severs thinks you're progressing very well."

"I'm sure getting bigger."

Hannah had reached the point where she finally felt that she *looked* pregnant. All the more reason to do the intimacy dance while she could maneuver. A couple more months might push Eric's desire a little too far.

But that was a worry for another time. Right now she simply wanted to bask in her happiness. She reached across the console and placed her hand on his thigh.

"I know you're really busy at work. Thanks for taking the time to escort me to the doctor."

"Not a problem. I had Jeanne reschedule my late-morning meeting for this afternoon."

What? She turned to look at him. ''You're going back to work?''

''After I drop you off.'' He glanced at her. ''Is that a problem? If you're able to get around yourself, I didn't think you'd need me hanging around this afternoon.''

She swallowed her disappointment. ''No. It's fine.''

She understood that he had responsibilities. Besides, it was wrong to blame him for not reading her mind. If she'd wanted him to take the afternoon off, she should have asked instead of just expecting him to know that's what she wanted.

Hannah prepared a simple dinner. She didn't want to tire herself by standing for too long. Not on her first day upright.

While the casserole baked, she curled up on the sofa and tried not to think about Eric. Not thinking about him also meant not watching the clock, not counting the hours, then minutes, until he pulled into her driveway. It meant not thinking about what was going to happen that night...in her bed.

She wanted him. Every part of her body was on fire for his touch. She wanted to feel him next her, inside of her. She wanted to please and be pleased. With a smile she wondered how well the casserole would keep if they didn't get to it right away.

A little after six, she heard his car. Excitement coursed through her as she rose and walked to the front door. She opened the door and was about to call out a greeting when she noticed the large suitcase he'd collected from the trunk.

"What's that for?" she asked as he walked into the house.

"My stuff." He paused to kiss her cheek. "I've been bringing it in a day at a time, but I figured I'd need a suitcase to get it all home. You don't want my suits taking up your closet space, now do you?"

Actually, she hadn't minded. She'd kind of liked seeing their clothes hanging side by side. Like they belonged together. Like she and Eric belonged together.

One thing she hadn't considered was that her clean bill of health meant that Eric didn't have to live with her anymore. Of course it made sense that he would want to return to his regular life, but did it have to be tonight?

"There's no rush," she said as he put down his suitcase. "You're welcome to stay as long as you'd like."

"Tempting," he said moving close and hugging her. "You're always tempting. While I appreciate the offer, I'm going to take the next couple of days to get caught up. I still have to work on my presentation for the interview. There's also a backlog from the hospital. I figure a few late nights will take care of things."

A coldness swept over her. She pulled free of his embrace and sank onto the sofa. "I don't understand. You want to leave?"

He shifted uncomfortably. "Hannah, it's not that I don't want to be with you. I do. But I have—"

She cut him off with a shake of her head. "I already know this part. Responsibilities. Your current job. Your potential new job as a vice president."

He frowned at her. ‘‘Why do you sound angry?’’

Did she? ‘‘Maybe because I am. I’m finally well enough to get out of bed, and I thought you’d want to be around for that. I thought you’d want to spend time with me.’’ She sucked in a breath as a possible truth occurred to her. ‘‘I thought you’d enjoyed our time together, but maybe I was wrong. Maybe all you felt was an obligation.’’

He crouched down in front of her and took her hands in his. ‘‘You can’t believe that,’’ he told her. ‘‘You know I like being with you. We have a great time.’’ He touched her cheek. ‘‘You have to believe that.’’

She wanted to—desperately. But she wasn’t sure about anything anymore.

‘‘Why is the job at Bingham Enterprises so important to you?’’ she asked. ‘‘Isn’t being the hospital’s youngest director enough? Do you need another promotion so quickly?’’

He rose and walked to the windows. ‘‘You don’t understand. My career is important to me.’’

‘‘I *do* understand. I know it’s important. I respect your goals. What I don’t get is why you can’t be balanced about your life. Instead you’re driven to succeed. What about growing as a person? What about friends? Lovers?’’

Me. But she didn’t say that.

‘‘Maybe I’m driven because I don’t have a choice,’’ he said, turning to face her. ‘‘We aren’t all lucky enough to have a trust fund to support us while we figure out what to do with our lives. Maybe if you didn’t have the Bingham fortune to fall back on you wouldn’t be so quick to judge me.’’

His words pierced her down to her heart. She flinched as if he'd slapped her. "Is that what you think of me? That I'm some shallow rich woman with no goals?"

"Aren't you saying *I'm* shallow? That all I care about is getting ahead?"

"Does anything else matter to you?"

His gaze narrowed. "I would think my presence here for the past week would be enough of an answer."

He had a point, but she was hurt and angry. She didn't care about that.

"Fine. So you're perfect and only you get to judge people, right?" She glared at him. "You want to know about my trust fund? Well, here's the truth of it. I've spent the last ten years of my life doing what everyone expected of me. Now I'm in a place where I can finally think about what I want. I'm not going to apologize for that."

"No one is asking you to," he said. "But what happens after the baby's born? What are you going to do with your life? You're smart, Hannah. You're talented and you could make something of yourself. Do you really have a plan or are you simply running away because that's always easier than facing the truth?"

"Oh, sure. Let's talk about what's wrong with me and ignore the issues of your life." She stood. "I thought you were different. I thought you could care about someone other than yourself, but I was wrong."

His expression tightened. "I'm sorry to disappoint you. This is who I am. If you can't accept that…"

Then what? Was it over?

Hannah clenched her hands together. A part of her wanted to yell at him to get out. She wanted to scream and give in to her temper. But the rest of her wondered if this was the right path. Didn't she love Eric? And didn't that mean trying to compromise?

She opened her mouth to say they both needed to calm down, when he walked toward the door.

"Forget it," he told her. "This was a bad idea from the start." He jerked his head toward his suitcase. "I'll be back in a couple of days to pick up my stuff."

Then he walked out the front door and was gone.

Eric made it home in twenty minutes, which gave him the whole evening to work on his presentation. But instead of hunching over his computer, he found himself pacing the length of his living room.

Nothing felt right. He hated the plain white walls and pale carpeting of his condo. As he paused by the sliding glass door and the view of town, he found himself thinking of Hannah's house. She'd put color everywhere. There were fabrics and textures and paintings.

"Idiot," he muttered, knowing it was safer to think about Hannah's house than the woman herself. Because thinking about *her* made him ache.

He crossed to the wet bar and poured himself a drink. As he sipped he tried to remember what their fight had been about. He wasn't sure. One second they'd been talking and the next...

The things they'd said to each other.

He hadn't meant to imply that she was shallow. He didn't think that at all. But she was so talented—

shouldn't she do something with her life? Something other than staying in the house with her baby?

Her words to him also echoed in the quiet room. She'd claimed he only cared about his career. He knew that wasn't true. Other things mattered. At least they used to. But lately...

Lately there hadn't been any reason to invest himself in more than his job. Was Hannah right? Her words echoed what his sister had always said—that he was losing himself in what he did. Was his job how he wanted to define himself?

But what about his goals, his dreams? He didn't want to give them up. Nor did he want to lose Hannah.

The truth slammed into him. He almost wasn't surprised.

Of course, he thought. That was the reason he'd pursued things even after he'd figured out she wasn't a good-time-only kind of person. He'd known she believed in happy endings and he'd kept on getting involved. Why?

Because he'd seen something in her he'd never seen in anyone else. He'd sensed she was the one person who could convince him love lasted and marriage worked.

He loved her.

Hell of a time to figure it out, he told himself. Right after yelling at her and stalking out of her life. So what was he supposed to do now?

Chapter Fifteen

Hannah spent a restless night. She tried to sleep for the baby's sake but spent most of the time staring at the ceiling. She replayed her conversation with Eric over and over, wondering what they could have said differently, what she could have done. She tried to assign blame, but gave up on that, figuring it was a fool's game.

Finally, shortly after six, she rose and showered, then sat in the kitchen over a cup of decaffeinated tea and tried to plan out her day, her week and maybe even her life. She had a feeling that all of them would be painfully Eric free. Which wasn't what she wanted.

So what *did* she want?

Hannah leaned back in her chair and closed her eyes. When she pictured her future, she pictured a toddler running across the grass, laughing. She pictured herself, pregnant again, but this time with Eric's baby. She pictured them together. Touching, smiling, happy. In love. But were her dreams possible?

Eric had his own future in mind and she doubted there was much room for a toddler or a second child. He wanted to be a vice president before he was thirty and a CEO shortly after that. He wanted long work hours. Relationships… She frowned as she realized she didn't know what he wanted from a relationship. Maybe one that didn't get in the way of his career dreams.

So where did that leave her? She'd vowed she wouldn't settle for less than a man who would love her with his whole heart and make her first in his life. She would do the same for him. But was that man Eric?

If it wasn't, then she was in trouble, because she'd fallen in love with him. Letting go of those feelings, getting over him, was going to take some time.

She mulled over her problem until shortly after seven thirty, when she heard a familiar car pull into her driveway.

"What on earth?" Hannah murmured as she walked to the front of the house and pulled open the door.

Eric was already climbing out of his car. He had a grocery bag in each hand.

"Good," he said when he saw her. "You're up. I didn't want to wake you if you weren't, but I didn't know how long the milk would stay cold."

As he approached, she automatically stepped back to let him in. Her battered emotions made it difficult to think. She wanted to throw herself at him. Or maybe yell at him. She also didn't understand why he was here.

"You went grocery shopping?" she asked, even as she drank in his handsome features. He looked good in his suit, but then he looked good in pretty much anything...or nothing.

"I knew you were low on a lot of things," he said as he set the grocery bags on the counter. "You've been in bed for a week and it's going to take some time for you to get your energy back. I didn't want you to push it. There's a store that opens early close to me. I figured I'd stop on my way to work."

They stood staring at each other. Hannah didn't know what to say. She wanted to hug him as much as she wanted to cry. The thoughtfulness of his gesture gave her hope, while the way he glanced at his watch and inched toward the door told her it was never going to work.

"Eric," she began. "I honestly don't know what to say. I'm not your responsibility. After last night, I never expected..."

He cut her off with a slight smile. "Hey, we're still friends, right?" He looked at his watch again. "I know we need to talk, but I can't right now. I have an eight-o'clock meeting that I can't miss."

She wanted to protest but held back the words. Instead she nodded, then walked him to the front door.

"I'll call you," he promised.

"Okay. Have a good day."

He waved and left.

When she was alone again, Hannah walked into the kitchen and began unloading the groceries. She was stunned by Eric's gesture. He'd taken the time to take care of her. That had to mean something, right? No man she knew ever shopped for groceries willingly.

Was there a way to blend what she needed and what he wanted? Could they find a way to make it work?

She supposed the answer to her questions lay in knowing how much she mattered to him. If he loved her, he might be more willing to compromise. If he didn't, then there was no point in continuing the relationship.

Oh, but the thought of being without him made her ache from the inside. He was a good man. Caring, affectionate, thoughtful, sexy. He knew what it was like to grow up without a father, and she believed in her heart that he would do his best to always be there for his children. She didn't think him not being the biological father of the child she carried would matter to him, either.

Eric was capable of great things, if only he would see that all his achievements didn't have to be inside the corporate world. But could she convince him?

She had to try, she told herself. She loved him too much to give up without a fight.

She would start today—by taking him out to lunch. They would talk and she would show him what their future could be.

Hannah dressed carefully, taking extra time with her makeup and hair. She arrived at the hospital shortly before noon and made her way to Eric's office.

Jeanne sat in her usual seat behind her desk. She grinned when she saw Hannah.

"You're mobile," she said, obviously pleased. "Walking looks good on you."

"Thanks. I got the all-clear yesterday. It's very nice to be back among the world of the upright." She nodded toward Eric's open door. "Is he expected back soon? I thought I'd surprise him by taking him to lunch."

Jeanne shook her head. "Sorry, Hannah. He's out for a couple of hours. Something unexpected came up, and he asked me to rearrange his schedule." She glanced around as if to make sure they were alone, then lowered her voice. "I'm probably not supposed to know this, but he's at Bingham Enterprises." She shrugged. "I'm friends with a couple of women in the Human Resources Department, and I recognized Carol's voice when she called to talk to Eric. I'm guessing he's over there for an interview."

Hannah felt heartsick.

"Don't worry," Jeanne said hastily. "I won't say anything to anyone. Eric's a great boss, and I'm completely loyal."

Hannah forced herself to smile. "I know you wouldn't get him in trouble, Jeanne. Thanks for telling me. I guess I'll just see Eric tonight." It was a lie, but a white one.

"Want me to tell him you stopped by?"

"No. That's okay. I don't want him to feel bad that he missed me."

If he would. That was the big question: Did she matter at all? Of course, if Eric was making a new life for himself, she already knew the answer. He was the kind of man who liked to travel light.

The pain in her chest was sharp and cold. In an

attempt to keep Jeanne from guessing anything was wrong, she said she had some errands to run and excused herself. On the way to the parking lot, she found it difficult to breathe.

Why had she let herself fall in love with him? Why hadn't she seen the truth? She blinked away tears and realized she *had* seen the truth—that was the problem. Eric was a good man. Kind, tender, caring. She'd thought that was enough, but it wasn't. She'd been so busy falling for him she hadn't stopped to realize he could never be what she needed—one hundred percent committed.

Her throat hurt and her eyes burned. Tears escaped down her cheek and she brushed them away as she hurried to her car. She was so intent on getting there, she didn't see the older woman who stepped into her path, and Hannah ran right into her.

They both nearly fell. Hannah reached for the woman's arm to steady her while grabbing hold of a car door to keep herself upright. It was only after they were both firmly back on their feet and she'd brushed the tears from her eyes that she recognized her grandmother.

"Hannah?" Myrtle said. "What are you doing here? Is it the baby?"

"No. I was going to see a friend, but he's out."

Her grandmother frowned, then touched her cheek. "You've been crying, dear. What is it?"

The concern in the older woman's voice was too much for Hannah and her hormones. She burst into tears and tried to sob out what was going on.

"I'm in love with Eric, b-but he doesn't want me. He only wants his c-career. Why can't the baby and

I be enough? I sh-should never have fallen for him, except he's the b-best man I know. I'll never love anyone else the way I l-love him."

Her grandmother shook her head. "Sounds like a big mess to me. Come on. We need to go somewhere and talk."

Myrtle ushered Hannah into her car, then drove back to the Bingham mansion. When they were both settled in Myrtle's sitting room, her grandmother leaned forward and smiled.

"Now start at the beginning, dear. Who is Eric and why has he broken your heart?"

Hannah clutched the glass of water she'd requested and started at the beginning. How she'd come back to town to settle down and had met up with Eric because the hospital was selling a house. She described her high school crush, how the boy had turned into a wonderful man and their mutual attraction. She left out the intimacy part because this was her grandmother, after all.

She talked about how cool Eric had been when he'd found out about the baby and how he'd taken care of her while she stayed in bed for a week. Then she talked about his ambition and the job at Bingham. When she was finished, she actually felt a little better, which surprised her.

"That's quite a story," her grandmother said. "I can see why you've fallen for your young man. Of course, ambition can be a double-edged sword. No woman wants to marry a man who won't take some responsibility for supporting the family, but too much emphasis on a career can make for a very lonely life for those left behind."

"Exactly," Hannah said. "I wish I could make Eric see that family life is important, too, but if I can't—" she swallowed a sob "—I guess it's going to be over between us."

Her grandmother stirred her tea. "Would you like me to call Ron, dear? I could talk to him and make sure Eric doesn't get the job at Bingham. That would solve your immediate problem."

Hannah half rose from her seat. All the feeling bled out of her hands and she could barely think. "What? *No!* Of course not. Grandmother, I may not be happy about Eric's decision, but I would never take away his choice. Besides, this is his *dream.* I don't want to be a part of his life just because he couldn't get what he really wants." She sank back in the chair.

"How interesting." Her grandmother sipped her tea, then looked at her. "Of course, you're going to be taking away his choice in a different way, aren't you, dear?"

"What?"

"You've said that the relationship is over because of Eric's ambition. You want him to want what you want, and if he doesn't, you'll end things. I've always thought compromise should be on both sides, but not everyone agrees with me."

Hannah opened her mouth, then closed it. No. Her grandmother had it wrong. She didn't want it all her way. Of course she was willing to compromise. She was a fair, giving person. She—

Her mind froze as she struggled to think of one way in which she'd been willing to compromise with Eric. She'd been upset about his leaving her to prepare for the interview. She'd been desperately hurt and had seen his actions as a portent for the future.

But had she asked for what she wanted? Had she suggested a compromise? Maybe there hadn't been a way to make it work, but she hadn't even attempted to find one. As for Eric, he'd reacted to her lashing out. She would never know what he would have done if she hadn't gotten mad.

"You seem to have a few things on your mind," her grandmother said.

"I do," Hannah said slowly. "I never thought of it that way before, but you're right. I have no right to ask Eric to change his dreams, and I never meant to, but isn't that what's going on? I need to tell him what I want, what I expect, then see if he's willing to work with me. Is there some middle ground for us?"

She looked at her grandmother and smiled. "If I love him, I should be willing to work to save what we have instead of assuming it's all over."

"It sounds like a good plan. Love is never easy. Both parties have to be willing to give 110 percent. That doesn't mean there won't be fighting, but the occasional argument can be a good thing. After you clear the air, you can kiss and make up." Myrtle smiled. "I hope I don't shock you by saying the making up can be very nice indeed."

Hannah spent the rest of the afternoon with her grandmother. They talked about family, Hannah looked at photo albums, and they connected in a way she would never have thought possible. By the time her grandmother dropped her off at the hospital parking lot, she felt clearer about a lot of things.

She stood by her car, then glanced up at the administrative offices. There was still a light on in one of them, and she decided this was as good a time as any to share her thoughts with Eric.

Jeanne was already gone. Most of the other staff members had left and the building was quiet. Hannah walked to Eric's half-open door and knocked.

He glanced up from his computer and seemed surprised when he saw her. Not to mention wary, although she couldn't blame him for the latter. The last time they'd talked for any length of time, she'd been pretty hostile.

"Hi," she said, walking into his office. "Got a second?"

"Sure."

He rose and motioned to the sofa. She followed him there and took a seat.

When he was next to her, facing her, but not close enough to touch, she drew in a breath.

Thousands of thoughts filled her head. She didn't know which one to voice first. Eric had been so good to her in a thousand ways. Weren't his actions important? Didn't they define the man he'd become?

And what about his questions about *her* future? She'd been upset by his talk of her not having goals, but she'd since realized he was right. She'd been enjoying law school right up until she'd gotten involved with Matt and had started feeling trapped by her life. Did she want to give that up? Couldn't she be a terrific mother and still have a career she enjoyed?

"You bought me food," she said, then had to laugh. "Sorry. That wasn't what I meant to say. It just came out."

His wary expression warmed. ''You already thanked me.''

''I know, but we had a big fight last night and you still took the time to go to the grocery store for me. That says a lot.''

''I wanted you to be okay. I worry about you.''

He looked as if he were going to say more. Hannah held her breath, hoping the *L* word might be involved, but he only shrugged. She realized then it was up to her.

''You were right, you know,'' she said. ''About me and law school. I do sort of miss it, and I would like to go back when the baby is older.'' She glanced down at her stomach. ''And born.''

He smiled. ''Sounds like a plan.''

''I want to have plans,'' she admitted. ''And a future I work for. I don't intend to spend the rest of my life living off my trust fund.''

''I never should have said that,'' he told her. ''I was angry, and I lashed out. I know you've worked hard, Hannah. You got into Yale Law School all on your own. You were doing well there.''

If his comments to her the previous night were his idea of lashing out, then there was definitely hope. Eric even fought fair.

''I was,'' she agreed. ''But I was also going crazy. I realize I've been swinging like a pendulum. For years I've done what I thought my family and my father wanted me to do. Suddenly I couldn't stand it and I was determined to do what I wanted instead. I wasn't going to listen to anyone. You pointed out that I have a responsibility to myself to make sure I'm doing what I want. I'd been so busy rebelling, I'd forgotten about that.''

''Happy to help,'' he said.

She sighed. ''Oh, Eric. I want to apologize for what I said last night. I was angry, too. But also hurt and disappointed. I thought after finding out the baby and I were going to be okay that you'd want to spend the evening with me. Maybe even the night.''

He looked surprised. ''I wanted that, too, but I thought you'd want to wait a couple more days just to be sure. I was afraid if I stayed, I'd push too hard.'' He gave her a half smile. ''And I was feeling some work pressure. I'd taken off a lot of time to be with you while you were off your feet, and I wanted to catch up. There was also the Bingham Enterprises interview.''

He'd wanted her! He'd been worried and acting thoughtful, not rejecting her. The news delighted her and made her long to stop their conversation and throw herself into his arms. Except she knew there were important issues still to be discussed.

''About your work,'' she said carefully. ''Sometimes I feel like that's all that's important to you. And that makes me sad. I like spending time with you, and I don't want that to stop.''

He slid closer and took her hands in his. His dark gaze settled on her face.

''I want that, too,'' he breathed. ''Hannah, you aren't the only one who has been doing some soul searching. I didn't sleep a whole hell of a lot last night, but I did figure out a few things.'' He paused. ''I've never been a big fan of love and marriage. My father was a real bastard, who broke my mother's heart. She never recovered and she never got over me being his son. CeCe was the one who raised me, until she left to get married. I was eight, and when she was gone, I felt completely alone. She explained that she was in love and getting married and that's why she had to go, but that didn't make it hurt any less.''

Hannah hadn't known about this. She clutched his hands. ''I'm so sorry.''

He shrugged. ''I got over it. But when CeCe and her husband split up, I was furious. She had left me for something that didn't even last. I started looking around and came to the conclusion that *love* didn't last. Nor did marriages. I decided the only thing I could count on was myself. I was determined to be a success.''

Her heart sank. Did this mean he didn't want her to love him?

''You are a success,'' she said.

''True, but at what price? You pointed out that I don't have a personal life. I've always been careful not to get involved. I didn't want the distraction. But you came along and I found myself caring. I wanted to be with you.''

He smiled at her. ''You've shown me a whole world I never knew about. One with caring and affection and love.'' He brought her hands to his mouth and kissed her fingers. ''I love you. I have for a while, now.''

She didn't know what to say. Her mind went completely blank. Finally she was able to blurt out, ''I love you, too. Oh, Eric, I want to make this work. I want you to have the career you've always dreamed of. I think the trick is for us to compromise, so we can each have our goals and a family, too.''

She realized what she'd just said. Loving her wasn't the same as wanting to marry her.

''I mean...''

He cut her off with a laugh. ''I know what you mean. I want us to be a family, too. I want to marry you and raise children with you. We already have a jump-start on that, but I think there will be a few more in our future. Agreed?''

She didn't know if he was asking about the baby, more children or the proposal, but she had the same answer for all of them.

''Yes!''

She flung her arms around his neck. At the same time he drew her close.

''Oh, Hannah. I love you,'' he whispered. ''I think I have from the very beginning. I just didn't see it.''

''Me, too. You're so amazing. Just the perfect guy.''

He pulled back a little. ''Hey, don't set me up with that. I'm far from perfect. But I'm trying to do the right thing for both of us.''

He kissed her, then touched her cheek. ''I had my interview at Bingham Enterprises today.''

''Oh. I'd forgotten. What happened?''

''They offered me the vice president job.''

''That's great. Congratulations. You must be very excited.''

''I didn't take it.''

She stared at him. ''I don't understand.''

He smiled. ''It's too much, too soon. Right now I'm not willing to put in that many hours. It would mean not seeing you or the baby enough. When I explained that, they offered me a director position. Less responsibility but still plenty of room for advancement. I told them I would think about it. I wanted to talk to you first.''

Hannah's heart was full to overflowing. She couldn't remember ever being this elated before. There didn't seem to be enough space in the world to contain her joy.

Eric loved her, and he wanted them to be a family. He cared about her, the baby, their future.

''Whatever makes you happy,'' she said. ''That's what I want.''

''You make me happy,'' he said, drawing her down on the sofa and wrapping his arms around her. ''Only you, Hannah. For always.''

Just as his mouth lowered to hers, she felt a fluttering inside her belly. It was barely a whisper of movement, yet she knew what it was.

''I felt the baby,'' she gasped. ''The baby's moving.''

She took Eric's hand and pressed it against the gentle flicker.

''Someone approves,'' he said.

''Our baby knows you're going to be a great dad. And so do I.''

Husband and father, Eric thought as he kissed her. Six months ago he would have laughed at the idea. But now he couldn't think of anywhere else he would rather be. He'd gotten lucky in love and lucky in life, and he planned to spend the next seventy or so years counting his blessing.

* * * * *

Don't miss the continuation of
MERLYN COUNTY MIDWIVES
Delivering the miracle of life...and love!

COUNTDOWN TO BABY
by Gina Wilkins
Silhouette Special Edition #1592
Available February 2004

BLUEGRASS BABY
by Judy Duarte
Silhouette Special Edition #1598
Available March 2004

FOREVER...AGAIN
by Maureen Child
Silhouette Special Edition #1604
Available April 2004

IN THE ENEMY'S ARMS
by Pam Toth
Silhouette Special Edition #1610
Available May 2004